FIZZ STUMP

THE BOY WHO RAN AWAY FROM THE CIRCUS

(AND JOINED THE LIBRARY)

A.F.HARROLD

ILLUSTRATED BY SARAH H

BURY

HI NEW YORK SYDNEY

L

For Daisy Yates

Bloomsbury Publishing, London, New Delhi, New York and Sydney

First published in Great Britain in 2012 by Bloomsbury Publishing Plc
50 Bedford Square, London, WC1B 3DP

A CIP catalogue record for this book is available from the British Library

ISBN 978 1 4088 3003 1

MIX
Paper from
responsible sources
FSC® C020471

Typeset in Great Britain by Hewer Text UK Ltd, Edinburgh

Printed and bound in Great Britain by CPI Group (UK) Ltd, Croydon CR0 4YY

7 9 10 8

www.bloomsbury.com

READERS SAY...

"It's funny, fantastic and ridiculous. I would put it in my top five books of all time, and I've read a lot of books – probably at least three thousand."

Milo, age 8

"Evil old people, a sea lion in a sparkly jacket and a lion called Charles with false teeth! What more could you want? I laughed my socks off."

Florence, age 9

"This book is like the 100 best books in the world put together!"

Hugo, age 10

"A great story that made me fizz with laughter!"

Felix, age 12

CHAPTER ONE

in which the hero is introduced
and in which he is described

There are many boys in the world, all slightly different from one another, and most of them are referred to by names. These are often John or Jack or Desmond, but sometimes they are James or Philip or Simon. Once, and once only, there was a boy whose name was Fizzlebert. (In actual fact, because, like most boys, he had a surname that came

after the Fizzlebert bit, he was known in full (for example, when someone was cross with him) as Fizzlebert Stump.) Most often he was just called Fizz.

So that you can get an idea of what this particular boy looked like, I'll tell you that he had unruly red hair. (To be fair, most boys have unruly hair, but only the especially brilliant ones have red hair.) He wasn't short for his height, and he knew how to juggle four balls at once, though not for very long. Usually he wore jeans and a t-shirt like most kids, but over the top he pulled on an old coat that the circus Ringmaster had outgrown. (Did I mention Fizz lived in a circus?) It was red with brass buttons, unpolished now, and in the rear it dangled down to the backs of his knees. It fitted pretty well because his

mother had taken it in at the waist and short-
ened the sleeves, but the shoulders with their
gold brocade epaulettes were still a bit broad
on him. To my mind (and to Fizzlebert's) it
made him look dashing, but to most people it
looked a bit . . . well, shall we say, silly?

Fizzlebert's mother was a clown. That's
not to say she messed about and made jokes

all the time (although she did), but rather that her job, the thing she was paid to do, was being a clown. The sort with a painted face, big trousers, long shoes, a bucket of white-wash, a ladder and an unfortunate sense of timing.

It was because his mother was a clown that Fizz lived in a circus. And also probably why he was called Fizzlebert, which is the sort of name only a clown would think of.

His father, on the other hand, was the circus strongman. A strongman is a chap who dresses up in a little leopardskin off-the-shoulder loincloth outfit, twirls his pointy oiled black moustache and lifts things up above his head to the marvelling applause of the audience. These things are usually awfully heavy things (the heavier the better), such as

great weights or huge boulders or bemused sea lions or particularly fat children from out of the audience who have been volunteered by their parents who believe such experiences are 'character building'. Occasionally he tried doing the act while lifting up smaller things, such as bunches of flowers, handkerchiefs or imaginary balloons, but the audience's reaction on those nights was never quite the same as when he picked up a child in one hand and a cannonball in the other, and started juggling them while whistling and dancing the cancan. (The cancan is a dance from France that involves kicking each of your legs up in the air one after the other. The best way to get the idea is to ask your parents or some other suitable grownup to demonstrate. There, see? Got it now? Super. I'll continue.)

Where have we got to?

There's a boy and he lives in a circus. What could possibly be wrong with this life?

Wrong? Why should something be wrong? Aha, well, here's something interesting about a story: if everything is alright, then there *is* no story: it's just a happy boy with happy parents. It's a good thing, for sure, of course, without

doubt, but it's not particularly exciting. So, let me share a secret with you . . .

Fizzlebert wasn't happy.

What? Living in a circus, getting to join in with the acts when they needed help? Hanging out backstage with clowns and acrobats and jugglers, with conjurors and fire-eaters and trapeze artistes, with escapologists and magicians and beautiful girls in sequins who ride the white horses with dazzling feathered head-dresses, with performing parrots and dancing dogs and prancing ponies all jumping through flaming hoops at the poot of their trainer's whistle? Getting to travel from place to place with the whole gang, waking up in a different town each day? How could he not enjoy that? The excitement! The thrills! The magic! The thrills! The excitement! (And so on!)

Well, truth be told, he wasn't very happy because there weren't any other kids living in his circus. He was the only one. His best friend was a sea lion. And not only are sea lions unable to play cards (instead of hands they have flippers, which are rubbish at picking things up) and are even worse at playing catch (they never throw the ball back, just balance it on their nose), but they're also lousy conversationalists. And they smell of fish.

And so this introduction opens (eventually) with Fizzlebert Stump sat out the back of the Big Top late one evening looking dolefully (which means sadly, miserably, gloomily and also slightly boredly) at a sea lion who has just burped a tuna-flavoured burp in poor Fizzlebert's face. And that's also where the

introduction closes, now that you've met the hero.

Let's hope the rest of the story gets more exciting.

CHAPTER TWO

in which a lion eats a child's
head and in which an audience
applauds tremendously

Fizzlebert Stump sat out the back of the
Big Top late one evening, feeling sorry
for himself. That evening's big perform-
ance had just finished. He'd put his head in
the lion's mouth and it had gone brilliantly.
The crowd were amazed. At first there was
a lot of clapping when the lion sat down and
growled. Normal people didn't often get to

see lions and so they were excited, but then when, at Captain Fox-Dingle's command, the lion leant forward and opened his mouth as wide as it would go the audience hushed down a bit. To a careful ear the noise they made was a bit confused. They were thinking 'this isn't much of a trick' and were wondering what was going to happen next. And then Fizzlebert stepped into the lion's cage. Some people shouted out warnings, because it's well known that lions and children shouldn't mix; some women fainted simply because they imagined what gruesome scene might happen next; and a small boy wet himself, with uncontrollable excitement.

By the time Fizzlebert knelt down beside the lion's vast open mouth and placed his head inside it, the audience had fallen as quiet as a

brick wrapped in cotton wool sat on a table in a sound-proof booth with all the lights out. As the seconds ticked by the circus band played a drum roll that wound the tension even tighter. (You know how when something's really tense people often say, 'Oh, I was on the edge of my seat'? Well, usually they don't actually mean it, it's just a figure of speech. This evening, however, as Fizz's head was stuffed between the lion's toothy jaws, two people in the audience were perched so close to the edge of their seats that they actually fell off and had to be given refunds. The Ringmaster didn't mind doing this when the tent was so full and the show so good. In fact, people falling off their seats was a sign that everything was going well, so long as they didn't *all* fall off, because that would have led to financial disaster.)

With his head in the lion's mouth all Fizzlebert could hear was the wafting wet wheezing of the lion's hot breath in his ears. It was damp and clammy and Fizz held his breath because it smelt of . . . well, whatever it smelt of was rather unpleasant. (Have you ever smelt a cat's breath just after it's eaten? A lion's breath smells much worse (for a

start, there's much more of it). My advice is: keep away from lions' mouths if at all possible.) Fizz had to keep his head in there for thirty seconds at least, until he felt the lion tamer's hand tap him on the shoulder. Then he stepped back, held his head up high and breathed deeply of the ever so slightly fresher air of the Big Top. He held his arms aloft (which just means up in the air, as if pointing toward the loft, except since the Big Top was a tent it didn't have a loft, but all the same he pointed to where a loft would've been had he been somewhere else) and listened as the crowd went wild.

The roaring and yelling and cheering and clapping went on for several minutes, so thrilling was the show. People had loved it.

Fizzlebert bowed forwards, then to the

right and then to the left. Everyone in the audience got a bow (those were the circus rules). He was tingling and buzzing all over. This was the best bit of the show. It more than made up for the lion's breath.

Charles, the lion, padded out of the circus ring and Fizzlebert followed him.

What the audience didn't know, and what you won't know until I tell you, is that this circus's lion was a particularly old one. Because Captain Fox-Dingle loved him very much, for years and years he had shared his after-dinner sweets with Charles. But because a lion is rubbish at brushing his teeth, after a few years they all fell out, and now the lion wore dentures. In fact it owned two sets. One set was hard and pointy and made for ripping and tearing, and Charles wore these when

ripping and tearing his dinner. The other set looked just as fierce, but were actually made of rubber and so were completely harmless.

After the rest of the show had finished and the audience had started going home, Fizz was sat just minding his own business on the steps of his parents' caravan. He was reading a book about dinosaurs in the light that spilt from the doorway. It was a warm night, summer was lazily oozing by, and he was getting a last breath of fresh air before bed, when suddenly he heard a voice shouting at him.

'Hey you!' it said. 'You were the one with the lion, weren't you?'

He turned around to see a gang of children running his way. There were five or six of them, some a bit older and taller

than him, some a bit younger and shorter. What he noticed immediately though was that they all seemed to be excited about something.

'You did that thing with the lion, didn't you?' asked the tallest of the bunch when they stopped just in front of him.

'Um, yes,' Fizz answered.

'You were brilliant, mate. Absolutely brilliant.'

'Oh. Thanks.'

'I thought you was gonna get your head ripped off. I reckon you must be really brave, eh?'

'It was very scary,' said one of the girls quietly.

'Yeah, I was so scared I wet myself,' said the smallest boy with obvious pride.

'Oh, I'm sorry about that,' said Fizz. He

certainly hadn't meant to spoil anyone's evening, let alone their trousers.

'No, it's alright. I don't care. It was amazing.'

'Yeah,' added one of the girls. 'Mum always brings a spare pair of pants for Billy. He wets himself at everything. Well, not everything, but anything he enjoys. I told her he's not really my brother. But Mum says he is and it's only polite that we keep him. But you . . . oh, you were wonderful.'

'Really?'

'Oh yeah. You were better than the clowns and the mind reader and the acrobats . . .'

She was interrupted by the girl who'd spoken quietly before. She spoke a little bit louder this time. 'I liked the dancing dogs best. They had pink tutus. I go to ballet.'

The other kids turned to look at her with open mouths.

'But I liked you a lot, too,' she added, turning quiet once again.

Fizzlebert had never spent a lot of time with kids his own age, because, as mentioned before, he was the only boy who travelled with the circus. He wasn't lonely, not really, because he had lots of friends among all the acts, but they were all grownups and some of them spent a lot of time being awfully serious. These kids were excited and exciting and they kept moving around as if they were nervous about something. And they liked Fizz. They'd said so. Maybe they could be his friends.

'I'm glad you liked the show,' Fizz said. 'Captain Fox-Dingle, he's the lion tamer, he'll

be dead happy when I tell him you thought our act was the best.'

One of the boys prodded one of the others with his elbow and the one who'd been prodded stepped forward (rubbing his side) and said, 'Hey, yeah? Well, we're having a game of football tomorrow afternoon. Um, do you . . .? Well, I mean . . . How'd you like to come and play? It's just a little kick around after school. You know?'

Wow! Fizz had never been invited to play football before. (He'd tried playing at the circus, but Fish, his sea lion friend, always balanced the ball on his nose, which was unhelpful at best.)

'Yeah,' he said excitedly, 'I'd love to! That'd be brilliant!'

'Smashing, we'll come and find you tomorrow, after school.'

'That's cool. When you get here just ask anyone where I am, they'll be able to find me.'

'What's your name then?'

'Oh yes! Sorry, I didn't say. I'm Fizzlebert, but everyone just calls me Fizz.'

Fizz held out his hand to shake, but the kids just looked at him.

'Fizzlebert?!'

The children, who a moment before had been in awe of Fizz, amazed at his stunt with the lion and hanging on his every word, now burst out laughing.

'What is it?' he asked, surprised at the sudden jollity. He wondered if there was a joke he had missed.

'Your name is *Fizzlebert?*' the tallest boy asked. 'Really? *Fizz? All? Bert?*'

'Ye-e-es,' said Fizzlebert, cautiously.

'That's the most stupid name I've ever heard!'

'It's just plain silly.'

'Ridiculous.'

'Stupid, stupid, stupid. Who ever heard of a boy called Fizzlebert?!'

Fizz was shocked. He didn't know what to say.

They'd seemed so nice, these kids. They had been interested in him and they wanted to be his friend, but now everything had changed. Instead of looking at him as if he were brilliant, they were looking at him as if he were something disgusting someone else had trodden in. (It's never much fun on your own shoe, but if you're mean-spirited and unpleasant then it's very funny when it happens to someone else.)

One of the boys did a little twirling dance like a not-very-good ballerina, singing, 'Fizzlebert Twizzlebert, Twizzlebert Fizzlebert,' over and over again in a silly squeaky voice.

All his friends laughed even harder at his dance and, as he spun round, the elder of the two girls slapped him on the back and sent him lurching giddily into the gang and they all fell over.

Fizz secretly hoped they'd hurt themselves, but they were up on their feet quick enough, brushing themselves down and wandering off into the darkness, still singing out his name and things that sounded a bit like his name. And laughing.

Maybe you've got a friend to go complain to when bullies pick on you like that, but

Fizzlebert Stump didn't. Not really. He didn't want to go and tell any of his grownup friends, because they were forever playing tricks and practical jokes on each other, calling each other rude names and generally taking the mickey. They wouldn't think Fizz being teased by some kids from the town would be a big deal. But, actually, he felt pretty rotten.

He sat back down on the steps of his caravan, with his dinosaur book shut on his lap (he had kept his thumb in his place just in case he wanted to read some more), and moped.

The sea lion, Fish, honked and waddled his way over and sat beside him with his head resting on Fizz's lap. He wore a spangly silver-sequined waistcoat and had long thick whiskers sticking out either side of his nose, which were glittery to match. He gazed up at

Fizz with enormous brown eyes. They were what anyone with a heart would call endearing. They always looked like they were about to cry, but never quite did, and had thick eyelashes that fluttered. They made you want to share things. Especially, Fish hoped, fish. They were eyes filled with a certain sort of love, the love that is called cupboard love.

Fish was a sort of friend to everyone at the circus, whether you lived there or were just visiting, so long as you had fish in your pockets. Fizzlebert didn't have any fish in his pockets and so after a few minutes Fish waddled off to look for someone who did, but not before letting out a moist fishy burp right in Fizz's face.

Just then a voice called his name from inside the caravan.

He recognised the voice immediately: it

was his mum. She was leaning out of the caravan doorway, looking at him sat below her on the steps. She was halfway through washing her face (the left half was still painted, the right half was clean) and she held a damp sponge in her hand. (If you've never seen a clown halfway in or out of his or her makeup, then I must say it's a weird sight. You know what a clown looks like, yes? And you know what a normal person looks like? Well, stick half of one face next to half of the other face and you'll see what I mean. Odd.)

'Fizz?' she called.

'Yes, Mum?'

'What was all that noise just now? It sounded like voices?'

'It was just some kids, Mum,' Fizz said.

'Some kid's mum? What did she want?'

'No, not some kid's mum, Mum. Some kids, Mum.'

'That's what I said darling,' she said, not really paying attention to his punctuation. 'What did she want? We're not the lost child desk. Did you tell her where it was?'

When Fizz's mum had taken off her clown

makeup and costume she stopped being funny. In fact, she was quite a serious woman most of the time. Not too serious to laugh, but serious enough to know that not everything is a joke. But right now with her makeup half on and half off, Fizz couldn't tell if she was trying to be funny or not.

'No, Mum. It wasn't anyone's mum. It was just a bunch of kids who saw me and came over.'

'Oh, what did they want? Did you tell them this isn't the lost property desk?'

'They didn't want the lost property desk, Mum. They came and said how good they thought the lion trick was this evening.'

'Oh, did you and Charles do your act tonight?'

'Yes, Mum. Didn't you see it?'

'No, I was trying to put the collapsing clown car back together, ready for the finale. You know how much trouble I have with that.'

'Oh,' said Fizz. He was a little upset that his mum hadn't watched his death-defying stunt with the lion. Of course, he knew she'd seen it before and, of course, they both knew it wasn't actually death-defying on account of the rubber false teeth, but all the same, he felt a little deflated. Any *normal* mum would watch her son put his head in a lion's mouth and be proud, wouldn't she? Any *normal* mum would have stuck up for her son when he was being teased.

But he had the feeling that if she'd come out when she'd heard the noise and told the kids off for calling him names and taking the mickey, they would've laughed at her even

more than they'd laughed at him. When a clown tries to be strict it always looks funny. People always laugh. And those kids would've been rolling on the ground clutching their sides, pointing at her and at him.

And knowing her, she would've thought they were laughing because they thought she was funny. But there are two ways of being funny, of making people laugh: one is by doing funny things on purpose (telling a joke or being a part of a comedy routine), and the other is by having people think you look ridiculous.

They were plain mean kids, it had turned out, and his mum would've just embarrassed him even more. If only he had a *normal* mum, who dressed in *normal* clothes that he could be seen in public with without everyone staring

and pointing. But she loved being a clown, he knew. It meant a lot to her.

'They liked the show?' she asked.

'Yes, I think so,' he said.

'They thought you were good?'

'They thought I was good, yeah.'

'Did they mention the clowns?'

'The clowns?' he asked.

'Yes, did they mention us?'

'Well, we didn't really talk for very long.'

'Oh well, I expect they liked the clowns,' she decided, pleasing herself.

'Probably,' he said.

'Well, Fizzlebert,' his mother said, 'I'm glad you're making friends.'

Then she was gone back inside.

'Friends,' Fizz said to himself, with a sort of grumbly sighing noise best spelled

~31~

something like 'harrumph' but pronounced however you like.

Not much later he went to bed himself, filled with the last little bits of excitement left over from the evening's show but with much more of the disappointment he'd got from those kids. Meeting them had been more exciting than the audience roaring, and when they'd gone away . . . why, that was crushing. He actually felt crushed.

And why had they gone? They'd gone, Fizz thought to himself as he lay in his bed, because he had a silly name. He just wished he was normal. Why did he have to live in a stupid circus?

And those were the thoughts rattling round his head as sleep finally overtook him and almost brought this chapter to an end.

But first there's a tiny flashback. Just before he went in for the night he stood up and stretched and noticed something on the ground where the kids had all fallen over when that boy had done his silly dance. It was a book. Fizzlebert liked books and so, in case it rained and the book got ruined, he took it indoors with him.

Now the chapter ends. There we go. That's it. It's stopped now.

CHAPTER THREE

in which a mind reader is met and
in which rabbits are discussed

The next morning Fizzlebert woke up in bed. This was a good start. Sometimes he woke up on the floor, which wasn't such a good start. It wasn't that he fidgeted in his sleep, but if the circus was travelling through the night then sometimes the caravan would sway on a sharp corner and if he'd forgotten to do up the buckles then he'd be tipped out on the floor. Fortunately the floor wasn't particularly hard and the fall wasn't particularly far, but on the whole everyone would agree it's nicer to wake up in bed than out of it. And that was exactly what Fizz thought too.

While he was sat in the caravan's tiny kitchen eating his breakfast (which was his usual candyfloss and cornflakes) he flicked through the book he'd found the night before. He could only assume that one of those horrible kids had dropped it. He didn't want to be accused of stealing the book, but he didn't know what to do with it. He had tried asking his mum, but she had already put her makeup on, ready to rehearse some new routines with the rest of the clowns, and she couldn't give a sensible answer.

'You could hide it in this bucket of custard,' she'd said, 'unless you're afraid of the sharks.'

That was typical of her. No help at all.

He wondered who else he should ask.

The book itself was a novel, and normally Fizz liked novels. He liked ones about adventures in outer space or in steamy jungles with dangerous animals, or with robots if at all possible. He'd read the first few pages and it was clear this novel had none of that. It was a story about life in a circus. Fizz thought a book ought to be an escape, ought to open a doorway into a different life for a few hours. This book didn't seem to do that at all. It just looked plain boring.

After breakfast Fizz had lessons. Even kids who live in circuses have to have some sort

of schooling (it's the law), but I dare say the classes Fizz attended weren't quite like the ones kids like you get at school.

All his different subjects were taught by different members of the circus. Each person taught Fizz the subject they felt they knew most about. For example, Madame Plume de Matant, the woman who told fortunes in a dimly lit and heavily perfumed tent by peering into a crystal ball (which was just an upside down goldfish bowl filled with purple smoke, but it looked all swirly and spooky and pretty mysterious): she taught Fizzlebert French. (Since Fizz didn't know any French to begin with, it didn't much matter that Madame Plume de Matant didn't know more than half a dozen words herself. A fortune teller, she thought, should be exotic and mysterious,

and so she had assumed what she called 'a French aura' years before, which involved eating croissants every morning, drinking too much coffee and saying 'oui' instead of 'yes' (which sounded like she said 'wee' a lot, which made Fizz laugh until she told him it actually meant 'yes' in French, and not 'wee'. That much she had right). The rest she made up and Fizzlebert never knew any different, not until the day he met a Frenchman, but that's another story entirely.)

Fizz's other teachers included: the Twitchery Sisters (*Mary and Maureen, the Human Trampolines*), a pair of acrobats, who took him for geography; Captain Fox-Dingle, the lion tamer, who gave him art classes; and Bongo Bongoton, one of the clowns, who gave him lessons in English, which was awkward

(which is to say, a bit silly) because he was a mime (and if you don't know what a mime is, I'd just keep quiet about it).

This morning however, Fizz had to go over to Dr Surprise's caravan for a history lesson.

Dr Surprise was the circus's *Mysterious Magical Mind Reader, Horrendous Horripilating Hypnotist and Incredible Invisible Illusionist*. (His job title was possibly the longest and most impressive in the whole circus but few people actually understood what it all meant.)

When Fizzlebert knocked on Dr Surprise's door Dr Surprise was surprised.

'What, eh? Who is it?' he shouted in his thin high voice through the open window.

'It's me, Fizz,' Fizz shouted back.

'Oh heck,' shouted Dr Surprise. 'Is it that time already?'

'I think so,' said Fizz, secretly hoping that maybe it somehow wasn't. He liked Dr Surprise, but he didn't like history.

'Okay, hang on. I'm just getting up. Give me a minute,' the man squeaked.

Fizz waited, scuffing his shoes in the dust and twiddling his thumbs.

In years gone by thumb twiddling was a popular way to pass the time, but these days it has rather fallen out of fashion. It just proves that Fizz hardly ever hung around with kids his own age. They'd have told him pretty sharpish that thumb twiddling was old hat and they'd have probably laughed at him like the kids the night before had when they learnt his name. But Fizz had grown up surrounded by grown-ups who were twenty, thirty, even forty years older than him and he'd picked up a few of their habits. They didn't mind thumb twiddling at all, in fact they would talk proudly of the days when one of their riggers won a bronze medal for it in the 1976 All-Circus Olympic-ish Games. (Riggers are the men who build the Big Top and take it down again every time the circus moves to a new town, and as a rule they're tough burly men covered with tattoos (tattoos are like drawings, but done by people who can't find any paper).)

Anyway, if you've never twiddled your thumbs then you don't know what you're missing. It's a brilliant thing. I do it. I expect your parents probably do it too. Certainly your grandparents. Next time you see them you should ask for a quick lesson. It'll only take a minute. It's dead simple. You just join your hands together in front of you, leaving

the thumbs untangled, and then you sort of let them chase each other round in circles. Easy, see?

You can do it for hours and hours and it's absolutely free and doesn't use any electricity and so is good for the environment.

Fizz, however, only had to do it for two minutes and forty-six seconds before Dr Surprise opened the door and invited him in.

Dr Surprise was a tall thin man. He wore a very dark suit, sharp and tight and oily, which squeaked ever so slightly when he moved. The stiff white cuffs of his shirt poked out of the bottoms of his sleeves and almost hid his hands from sight. What you could see of his hands was covered by thin black silk gloves. He was bald except for a few long strands of hair that grew from somewhere near the back and looped around the dome of his head several times before drooping pointily downwards just above his left eye. His moustache was impressively curly, a deep midnight black, and from a particularly expensive Christmas cracker.

In his right eye he clutched a monocle (that's like half a pair of glasses, in case you didn't know) that glinted whenever he moved his head, which he didn't do very often at all.

On his feet were a pair of large pink fluffy slippers shaped like rabbits. (When he went on stage he changed into smarter shoes, but right now he was off duty.)

He smelt ever so slightly of wax.

'So,' he said when they had sat down at the little table they used for lessons, 'what are we to study today?'

'I think,' said Fizz, 'that we'd just got up to the Wars of the Roses.'

'Aha!' shouted the Doctor in his high warble. 'I knew that!'

(Well, he was a mind reader after all, so it wasn't all that surprising that he knew.)

'So what happens next?' asked Fizz.

'I think there was another war. Didn't you read the next chapter in the history book?'

'Well, no, because you set fire to it last week. Don't you remember?'

'Set fire to it?'

'Yes, you were showing me how to do the trick where you make sparks come out of your fingers.'

(Fizz always tried to get the Doctor to teach him tricks. It was better than learning history, and probably more useful too.)

'Ah, Brilliant Brewster's Bright Bedazzler?'

'That's it,' Fizz said.

'And that set fire to the book?'

(Fizz didn't mention that he'd 'accidentally' left the book out just where they were doing the trick. He liked books, as I've already said, but not *all* books.)

'Yes,' Fizz said. 'And then you said not to panic, because you'd get another one.'

'I did?' asked Dr Surprise, cautiously.

'Yes, you were going to go shopping.'

'Ah. Well. I never quite got round to it. I've been busy, you see.'

'Busy?'

'Yes, I've been thinking about setting fire to my hat. A tall blaze of flames winding up from within. What do you think?'

'Isn't that dangerous?' Fizz asked.

'Oh no. Not at all. I've mostly worked it out. I lift my hat, turn it over, hold it away from me, run my hand over it and woosh! A pillar of flame bursts ten feet into the air. Spectacular! It's basically the same as the Brewster's Backfiring Blaster-Bomb, but on a larger scale. Only,' he added, 'I must remember to do the fire trick *after* I've pulled the rabbit out. Otherwise . . .'

'It's cooked rabbit for dinner?' Fizz asked mischievously.

'No, no!' Dr Surprise squeaked in a pretend frenzy. 'You nasty boy. How dare you suggest such a thing? I couldn't eat Flopples. She's been a friend to me for more years than I can count on one hand.'

'Six years?' Fizz suggested, knowing that Dr Surprise always counted with his fingers.

'No, more years than I can count on my left hand.'

'Ah, five years then?'

'Yes. For five years Flopples and I have been best friends, comrades in magic, associates in otherworldliness. She has helped my shows soar to their great heights and no one can take that away from her.'

Flopples, as you'll have realised, was the

rabbit that Dr Surprise pulled from his hat halfway through the show. You might also be wondering what happened to the missing finger on his left hand, but all I'll say about that is: be *very* careful if ever you try training a rabbit with a carrot that's too short.

They discussed this new trick for a while before Fizz started asking Dr Surprise about hypnotism. (He always asked Dr Surprise about hypnotism because it was Fizz's favourite bit of the Doctor's show.) It seemed the Wars of the Roses had been completely forgotten.

Hypnotism is the art of putting someone into a 'state of suggestion'. That means that they'll do whatever you ask them to, even if it's something quite silly, like hopping on one leg or pretending to be a cat or even pretending to be a cat that's hopping on

one leg. That's exactly the sort of thing that makes an audience laugh nervously (it's very funny, just so long as it's not you that's been hypnotised).

Fizz had seen the show many times. He'd watched Dr Surprise slowly and steadily swing his pocket watch to and fro and laughed at how the perfectly ordinary normal boring

people out of the audience would do what he said. It looked so simple. 'Just concentrate on my watch,' he would say, 'you are getting sleepy,' and they'd answer and say, 'I am getting sleepy.' And then he'd say, 'When I count to ten you will obey only my voice.' And then he would count up to ten and the person would say, 'Yes, Master,' (he always asked them to call him 'Master' because it was scary and scary is good for business). Then he would say, 'When I snap my fingers you will wake up and remember nothing of what has happened.' And after he'd had them pretend to be dogs and jump through hoops or pretend to be chickens and scratch at the sawdust looking for grain, he'd snap his fingers and they'd say, 'Have you started yet?' not realising that he had not only started but

also finished, and they'd go and sit back down thinking nothing had happened, until their friends told them all about it later on.

Fizz thought it was brilliant and funny and also a bit scary, and he'd been badgering Dr Surprise to teach him the trick for months, but the Doctor was very careful about not revealing all of his secrets.

'Go on,' Fizz said today.

'No, I cannot reveal my powers to you, Fizzlebert Stump. They bring me a great responsibility and I must keep them hidden, for fear they might fall into the wrong hands of some evildoer.'

'Oh, go on, it's only me.'

'No. I cannot. Now, I think, this lesson is over. Look, it is almost eleven o'clock. I must begin rehearsing the new trick.'

'Setting fire to your hat?'

'Yes. So, you'd best run along.'

'Okay,' Fizz said. 'Bye then.'

But Fizz lingered in the Doctor's doorway, one foot on the steps and fresh air already in his lungs. And there he paused, just for a moment. He had wanted to ask Dr Surprise for some advice, but had forgotten until now. It was only when leaving the caravan that he'd picked up the book he'd found the night before and had remembered. But Dr Surprise wanted to be getting on with his new trick, and Fizz didn't want to delay him any longer.

As he hesitated, the Doctor raised a finger in the air with a mysterious flourish, and said, 'Wait! I sense that there is something you wish to ask me, yes?'

'Well . . .' Fizz said.

But before he could ask his question Dr Surprise spoke again.

'You want to know about that book? Yes? Am I right?'

'Wow,' said Fizz, quite amazed. 'How on earth did you know that?'

'Well . . .' said the Doctor, smiling widely under his tiny moustache.

(Of course, Fizz shouldn't have been surprised at all. I mean, he knew that Dr Surprise was a mind reader. But also, he might have noticed that he had been clutching the book and lingering as if to say, 'I want to say something about this, but I'm not sure I should'. (I'm just saying, it's worth remembering that it doesn't always take a mind reader to read a mind.))

Fizzlebert told him the story of how he'd found the book, though he didn't mention about how the kids had taken the mickey out of him before running away laughing.

'Well, let me see,' Dr Surprise said, taking the book from him. 'Ah, look. Do you know what this is?'

He had opened the front cover and there pasted inside the book was a flap of paper with two columns of dates stamped in blue ink. Fizz had wondered about that earlier, but didn't know quite what to make of it.

'This is a library book. You see these dates? They tell you when the book has to be taken back.'

'Taken back where?'

'Back to the library.'

'What's a library?' asked Fizz.

(Now, of course *you* know what a library is, and you're probably thinking that *everyone* knows what a library is, but you have to remember that Fizzlebert had grown up in a travelling circus. He had never lived anywhere long enough to learn about a library, let alone to join one and borrow books. So please don't think him stupid for not knowing. I mean, I bet you don't know what a *corde pareille* is, but Fizz did. (It's a circus act in which the performer does spectacular graceful astonishing acrobatic things on a rope that hangs straight down from the highest point of the Big Top.) So now you know, and now Fizz is learning about libraries. Everyone's learnt something. What a very useful book this is.)

'It's a place where books are kept,' said the Doctor, explaining about the library. 'You

say you only met the boy whose book this was briefly? And you don't know where he is now? Well, there's only one thing to do, isn't there?'

'Is there?'

'Yes. This book is due back tomorrow and if it isn't returned to the library your new friend will be in trouble.'

'In trouble?'

'Oh yes. It's a serious thing having a book out too long.'

'Is it?'

'Oh yes. Very serious indeed. What if someone else wants to read this? What would happen then?'

'I don't know.'

'No. And neither do I. Very serious.'

'What can we do?'

'*We* do nothing, Fizzlebert. I have a trick to practise. *You*, on the other hand, should take this book back.'

'Back to the boy who . . .?'

'No. You said you don't know where he is. No, you'll have to take it back to the library for him. Do a good deed.'

Fizz didn't like the idea of getting the boy into trouble, even if he had been mean. That wouldn't really be fair and although he was unhappy, he didn't want to be nasty. So, yes, he thought, he would take it back, but . . .

'But, Dr Surprise, I don't know where this library is either.'

'Ah, that's easy,' the Doctor said. 'Look, the address is written in the book and it's not very far at all.'

The two of them climbed down from the

caravan and walked to the edge of the circus tents.

Dr Surprise pointed to the other side of the park.

'You see there, just round the duck pond and up that path?'

'Yes?'

'Well, through those trees is a little road and the library is the building just on the right. It's a five-minute walk from here.'

'So, it's past the duck pond, up the path through the trees and you say it's just on the right?' Fizz repeated. 'How will I know which one's the library?'

'It will say "Library" over the door in big letters. Be full of books. You can't miss it. Just go in and give the book back. That's all you have to do.'

'That's all I have to do?'

'That's all. It won't take you more than ten minutes all told. But first . . .'

'First?' asked Fizz.

'You'd best tell your parents where you're going. We don't want you getting in trouble, do we?'

Before Fizz could answer Dr Surprise spun on his rabbit-slippered heel and headed off back to his caravan where his new trick was waiting to be tried out.

Fizzlebert began walking across the park, down past the duck pond and towards the trees on the far side behind which hid this library place. The tails of his frock-coat fluttered as he walked and the cool breeze of the late summer morning ruffled his red hair like the hand of an over-friendly aunt.

He looked back at the circus once. All the tents and caravans and lorries looked so small next to the enormous Big Top with its orange and yellow stripes shining bright in the morning sun.

For just a second he wondered whether he should do as Dr Surprise said, and go and tell his parents, but his mum was wearing her clown face now and she would just crack another stupid joke if he tried to tell her anything, and the last time he saw his dad he'd been trying to work out how a man could lift a horse.

Fizz had tried telling his dad things before, but he usually became distracted and dropped whatever it was he was lifting. Fizz didn't fancy being responsible for his dad dropping a horse. (The woman in charge of the horses

(Miss Tremble) was the sort of person who cried when one of her horses had its hair cut. Who knew how she'd react if the strongman dropped one of her prize ponies. Fizz didn't want to find out.)

'Anyway,' he said to himself, 'I'll only be ten minutes. They won't mind me popping out for that long.'

Of course, Fizzlebert's parents didn't mind him popping out, but only because they didn't know about it. By the time Dr Surprise had set fire to his hat a few times he'd almost completely forgotten the morning's lessons, and besides he *had* told Fizz to tell his parents, so it wasn't his fault, was it?

Hang on, what wasn't his fault? Fizzlebert

is just taking a book to the library and coming straight back, isn't he? We've all done that, haven't we? It's easy. What could possibly go wrong?

CHAPTER FOUR

in which a librarian is encountered
and in which death robots from
Mars make a brief appearance

Fizzlebert was about to push open the door
to the library when it opened all by itself.
It trundled to one side and waited for him to
step through. To Fizz this was unusual. Circus
tents don't have automatic doors and neither do
caravans. He was startled, but he wasn't scared.

In an earlier age a boy faced with an automatic sliding door, a door that seemed to think

for itself and which knew when someone was coming, would think it was witchcraft or black magic. They'd run and hide, rather than step through the doorway the devilish door was offering. Maybe they'd call the police or a priest to come and examine the door for demons and ghosts. But Fizz lived, more or less, now (or, at least, not so many years ago) and he understood about things like motors and electronics. He listened to the radio and had even been to the cinema a few times, and a door that could trundle out of the way when someone walked towards it didn't seem an impossible thing.

It wasn't the magic door that made him pause on the doorstep, but the responsibility he'd taken upon himself. He held the library book in his hand and he could hear Dr Surprise's voice in his ear saying, 'Just hand it in.' But he didn't know exactly what was going to happen in there. Would he have to explain where he'd got the book? Might the person behind the counter start asking him questions he didn't know the answer to?

That's what made him nervous.

As he hesitated the automatic door began to slide shut again. 'Trundle, trundle,' it went.

Fizzlebert stepped backwards and the doors stopped closing and began opening yet again, trundling in the opposite direction.

He grabbed the opportunity and scrunched up his courage and stepped through, saying, 'Thank you,' to the door that had done its job so well.

Inside it was nice and cool. It was spacious and brightly lit. Directly in front of Fizzlebert was a woman sat behind a wide desk. Her face was round and plump and red-cheeked and she looked a little out of breath. She wore a pair of glasses on the top of her head, rather than on her eyes, as if she had a secret pair of eyes under her hair that were watching the ceiling closely, and she was chewing the end of a biro. There were blue ink stains round her mouth.

A badge pinned to her grey-green cardigan

(which seemed to be a size too small, as the buttons strained to keep it shut across her chest) said her name was 'Miss Toad'. (Fizz was too polite to think to himself, 'How appropriate,' or if he did think it he was too polite to ever tell anyone he had thought it, which pretty much amounts to the same thing.)

Behind her, beyond the desk, filling up the rest of the tall building, were shelf after shelf of books. Fizz had only once or twice ever been in a bookshop, when he'd gone shopping with his dad. He'd been allowed to pick one book under five pounds on each shopping trip. He remembered what he'd bought. They'd been brilliant books. One was a collection of funny poems and one was a book about frogs. Fizz had read them both many times. 'Did you know,' Fizzlebert might ask you if you met him, 'that some frogs have sticky pads on their feet so they can climb up trees? Or that frogs shed their skin from time to time? Or that when they shed their skin, they first loosen it by wriggling around and then pull it up over their heads as if taking off a jumper, and then eat it?' Did you know that? Well if you didn't, you do now, and that's because that little frog book had been one of Fizz's favourites when he was six years old.

'Can I help you?'

(That was Miss Toad speaking. She had a grumbling rumbling raspy deep voice which almost sounded like she was burping the words she spoke. But Fizz knew that she wasn't actually burping her words, because grownups don't do things like that. Well, not

very often, and *never* when children might hear.)

Fizzlebert walked over and gave her the book he'd found.

'Someone said I should give this to you,' he said, hoping that would be enough explanation.

'Thank you,' she said.

She turned the book round to face her, opened it up and waved a red light over the front page. There was a beep from her computer. She looked at her screen and said, 'That's fine.'

Fizz didn't know what to do now. She hadn't asked any complicated questions and the book had been given back. But . . .

He looked at the shelves and shelves of books and wondered.

'Are these all yours?' he asked quietly.

'Well,' Miss Toad smiled, inkily, 'they're not *mine*, are they? They belong to the library. Is that what you mean?'

'Um, yes?'

'Yes, those are all our books. Well, some of them. There are more upstairs,' she rumbled.

She looked at Fizz's face. It was like the sort of face that you sometimes see in books of old photographs pressed up against a sweet shop window. Except the boys in those sorts of pictures are normally in black and white and wearing little school caps. But the eagerness, the desire to be let in was the same.

'The children's section is through the arch over there,' she said, pointing round the corner. (Pointing round corners is a really

good trick and quite easy to do if you have long enough arms.)

'Can I have a look?'

'Of course,' she burped. 'Go on.'

Forgetting that he'd told himself he'd only be ten minutes taking the book back, and forgetting that he hadn't told his parents where he was going, Fizzlebert thanked Miss Toad and, smiling, walked deeper into the library.

Bookcases loomed up into the air on either side and the smell of the room became more papery, slightly musty, ever so friendly. The carpet felt deep under his shoes and comfortable and quiet.

Threading his way through the tall stacks he found the arch the lady had pointed to and stepped through into a smaller, more colourful room. The shelves in this room were lower. He could reach the books on the top of the bookcases and he liked the look of them.

The room was empty. Empty of people, that is; obviously it was jam-packed full of books. There were also some chairs and tables and a whole corner had been given over to beanbags and a big wooden caterpillar which had shelves in it and provided a home, it seemed, for big flat picture books. But other than all that sort of stuff, the place was empty of people. It was a Tuesday and although it was the summer, term hadn't quite wound up and was only thinking about ending, so normal kids were still in school. So, this morning, Fizzlebert was the only boy in the whole library.

The room was full of more books than he'd ever seen in his life. Brilliant! Amazing! Just looking along one shelf at random and reading the titles, it seemed that every single book was different. Where to begin?

He shut his eyes and pulled out the first book his hand fell on. The title was: *The Great Zargo of Ixl-Bolth and the Flying Death Robots of Mars*. He tried saying the unfamiliar words and after just two goes he thought he could pronounce them properly. Reading the back of the book it said it was about a big war between two alien races . . . and yes, it had robots (flying ones (from Mars)). Well, if that wasn't right up his alley (which is a different way of saying 'if that wasn't his cup of tea', which I didn't say because Fizz didn't drink tea, preferring hot chocolate or cold squash) then he didn't know what was.

He looked at the price that was printed at the bottom of the back cover, just next to the barcode.

Looking in his purse, he had just enough money to buy the book.

They would only be in this town another couple of days before the circus moved on, and he might never find his way back to this library and he really wanted to find out what *The Great Zargo* was.

He quickly made a decision.

'Excuse me,' he said a minute later to the lady at the front desk, 'I'd like to buy this book please.'

He handed her the book and started to empty his purse out onto the counter top.

'*Buy* this book?' Miss Toad asked, the words rolling out of her inky mouth like curious boulders.

'Yes please,' he said.

'But you don't need to *buy* the book. This is a *library*.'

Please, don't laugh at Fizz. I know that you know and you know that I know that you know how a library works, because we've

been to them and we've all borrowed books. Sometimes we borrowed them for fun, sometimes to do some homework. Sometimes we had to get a book out or take one back for our granny. The important thing to remember is that we've been there and done it. Fizzlebert, as I said in the last chapter, had *never* been to a library before. He wasn't to know how they worked. Naturally, looking around at all those books, he thought the place was just a big bookshop.

Imagine how surprised he was when she told him he could borrow the book and didn't have to pay anything. How brilliant is that?

'What?' he said. 'You mean I can just have it?'

'No,' she rumbled, 'but you can borrow it.'

'Are you sure I can borrow *this* one?'

'Yes, of course.'

'But are you sure about *this* one?' He wondered if she was making it up, or if there was a special offer on certain selected books.

'Yes, you can borrow them *all*. Well, only four at a time, but . . .'

'I can borrow them all?' he said, his mouth falling open. He looked around at the shelves, tall and dark and looming, but filled to the brim with books. More books than he could ever imagine reading in an entire lifetime, and he could just *borrow them all!*

'Yes, you can borrow *any* of them,' Miss Toad went on. 'All I need to do is scan your library card and stamp the book and it's yours for the next four weeks. You can leave

this one here for the moment and go and choose some others if you like. I'll keep it safe for you.'

There was something in what she just said which had caught hold of Fizz's ears, something that he'd heard but hadn't quite understood. What was it?

'Library card?' he said, after a moment.

'Yes, your library card,' Miss Toad said. 'The card that says you're a member of the library.'

'A member of the library?'

She leaned over the counter to look at him closer. Her big round face loomed like the bookcases had, and her glasses slid down from her hair, over her forehead to land, plop, on her nose. Her eyes became enormous. The lenses were very thick. The ink stains round her mouth moved weirdly as she talked.

'Are you not a member of the library?'

She pointed at him with the grizzled end of her biro.

Fizzlebert quaked. Here came the hard questions. He had known something was going to go wrong, that there was going to be a catch, and here it came.

'No?' he said, making it sound a bit like a question just in case she knew better.

'Well, you'll want to join then, won't you?'

She smiled in such a way that her cheeks wobbled like two blue-spotted jellies. It was her way of being friendly, he decided.

'Yes, I think so. Is it complicated?'

'No it's very easy,' she burped.

Fizz felt relieved.

She reached under her desk and brought out a folder with some forms in and tapped at the top one with her pen.

'Now,' she said, 'are you over sixteen years old?'

If Fizz had been a less polite boy he'd have looked at her as if she was stupid.

'No,' he said, surprised that she hadn't been able to tell.

She put her pen down and laid her plump ink-stained hands either side of the sheet of paper.

'In that case,' she said, 'your parents will need to fill in the form. Are they around?'

Fizz mumbled something that might've been a 'no' but which also might've been a 'yes'. He knew they weren't around, but he didn't want to admit it to her.

He'd had his heart set on this book, and now he couldn't have it. He wanted to bang it down on the desk and stomp out, but he stopped himself from making a scene. His eyes began to fill with tears and he felt angry with himself for almost beginning to sort of cry. It was only a book after all.

(I'm sure you know what it's like when you've been really looking forward to something that, at the last minute, doesn't happen. Even if it's no one's fault you can still feel rotten about it inside. You feel like you want to cry or shout or throw a hissy fit, even though you know no one's to blame and no one's been mean to you. Well, Fizz felt something like that.)

He left the book on the desk and walked out the library door.

It opened for him with a grumbling trundle, and with his head down and his mind full of unfair thoughts he forgot to say 'thank you'.

He would have to go back to the circus now.

His parents were awfully busy rehearsing and practising their shows, and when they weren't doing that they were usually helping someone else with their rehearsals, or they were doing odd jobs round the circus. Everyone mucked in on cleaning up, for example, and the Big Top had to look good before the show.

Even if he did ask them they probably wouldn't have time to come all the way here to sign the forms. And if he asked them to, he'd have to confess that he'd come to the library without their permission in the first place, and he'd definitely get in trouble for that. But he wouldn't get in trouble if they didn't know he'd gone and the only way they wouldn't know was if he didn't tell them. But if he didn't tell them, then he'd never get to join the library.

Fizzlebert was caught in something of a pickle. He didn't know what to do for the best.

Wiping away his tiny tears he grudgingly began down the road toward the trees, through which the path led back to the park. There wasn't a lot else he could do.

But as he started off a voice behind him called, 'Little boy, do wait a moment, won't you?'

He turned round and there was a little old lady stood outside the library waving at him. Beside her was a gentleman he assumed was her husband. They were both very short, not much taller than he was.

The old woman walked towards him.

'We couldn't help but overhear what you were saying to the lady in there,' (she gestured behind her towards the library) 'and we wondered if we might be able to help. You did look sad.'

And it's there that this chapter stops.

Who are these old people? How might they be able to help? What will Fizz do next?

These questions are the sort of things an author dangles at the end of a chapter in the hope that they will make you want to read the next one, in order to find out the answers. It's an old trick.

I do hope it still works.

CHAPTER FIVE

in which two old people are met and
in which a kindly favour is done

So, you've come back? That's good. This is one of the more dramatic chapters in the book. It's quite a good one. I think you'll like it.

If you remember Fizz was outside the library after having just found out that he couldn't join up (and borrow brilliant books) unless he came back with his parents. And he couldn't ask his parents to sign him up because he hadn't told them he was going to the library. So he had just resigned himself to a future leading a library-less life.

However, as he was about to walk away an old lady called out to him and offered to help. This is where we pick up the story.

'Little boy,' the old lady said, 'Arthur and me, we can't bear to see such a little angel as you, you poor little thing, wander away unhappy. You look so down, so sad, so lost. Might we be able to help, do a good deed for you?'

Fizzlebert wondered what she meant.

She looked about the same age as his grandmother. (In case you were wondering, his gran had retired from circus life and now lived in a caravan park by the seaside (which is why she's not in this book).) This old lady had a back curved a bit like an upside down L (or a right way up 7), and if she were straightened out she'd have been much taller than Fizz was. As things were she was about the same height. Her face was wrinkly at the edges and her mouth was small and puckered and painted pink. Her eyes stared out from the

middle of carefully applied green smudges and her cheeks were soft and red and fuzzy like peach skins. Sprigs of blue hair poked out from underneath a little hat shaped like a round chocolate box. It was a shade of purple which clashed horribly with her hair and face. Her coat and shoes were the same colour. She squinted at him from behind the smallest pair of glasses Fizz had ever seen. They were clipped to the end of her pointy nose and she had to lean her head back and peer down the length of her long face if she wanted to look at him properly.

Her husband was shorter than she was. Or rather he would have been if she'd stood up straight. With her back bent like it was, they were about the same height. He had two enormous ears (one on either side of his head) which

whistled from time to time as his hearing aids played up. (There's no way Fizz could possibly have known this next fact, but I'm going to tell you it anyway, just because I think it's an interesting thing to know: when the old man held his head at a certain angle his hearing aids picked up the horse racing on the radio. The precise angle at which this happened made him look like he was thinking deeply, and because he usually closed his eyes in order to picture the race better, people often mistook him for someone who was frightfully intelligent and full of deep thoughts. For the most part, though, he wasn't either of those things. He just liked horses.)

As well as huge ears, the old man had a great big nose too (right in the middle of his face, unsurprisingly). This didn't whistle.

Underneath his nose was a bushy moustache which drooped down over his mouth. Where the moustache met his nose it was hard to tell which hairs belonged to the moustache itself and which ones snaked down out of his nostrils. They all seemed to twine together as one furry mass, and from time to time they tickled him so much that he sneezed, and a sneeze so close to a moustache as bushy as that (especially if the sneezer had a cold at the time) is not something you want to think about. Really, don't think about it. Really.

Fizzlebert thought he glimpsed a bit of toast dangling in a web of hair by the corner of his mouth (not a whole slice of toast, of course, just a large crumb), but he couldn't be sure. He tried his hardest not to stare. (Fizz was a polite boy, when he remembered.)

The old man was wearing a scarf tucked into a brown overcoat, even though it was a warm summer day. On the top of his head, above a few wispy strands of grey hair, was a battered little trilby (which is a sort of hat). It seemed to be too small for his head (definitely too small for those ears) and he was forever reaching up to make sure it was still on.

These were the two people Fizz faced.

'You can help me?' he said.

'Maybe,' the woman replied.

'How?'

'You need someone to vouch for you.'

Fizz didn't know what 'vouch for' meant, so he said, 'Do I?'

'Yes! You need someone to say you are who you say you are. I thought I heard Miss Toad say you needed your parents to help you join the library. Is that right?'

'Yes,' Fizz said.

'Well, I suppose you're just off to find them now, aren't you?'

'Um, well, no . . . they're . . .'

'What?'

'Too busy,' Fizz said. Telling part of the truth.

The old woman looked at him closely through her vertiginously balanced spectacles for a moment.

'That's not all, is it?' she asked. 'You can tell me . . .'

When Fizz said nothing (he didn't know what to say), she stepped closer and pulled another pair of glasses out of her handbag. These were on a little stick, so that instead of looping the arms round her ears and letting

them rest on her nose (like you would do with ordinary glasses), she held them out in front of her and moved them backwards and forwards to get him into focus.

Peered at through two pairs of spectacles Fizz felt he was under uncomfortably close scrutiny.

He scuffed his feet in the dirt and thought that maybe he should be leaving.

'Your parents don't know you're here,' she said suddenly.

Fizz nodded.

'Oh, you poor thing,' she went on, 'left to wander, uncared for and all alone. I can't bear to see a little chap like you dangling dolefully at a loose end like this, abandoned and forgotten. Let us help you.'

The old man looked thoughtful and closed

his eyes, as if he was thinking about what good deed they might be able to do for the poor boy.

'I tell you what,' she said, putting the second pair of glasses back in her handbag, 'we shall pretend to be your parents for you. That way you can join the library and get your lovely library card. And then you can borrow as many books as they will let you and go home and read them all to your dear heart's content. What do you say, you poor boy? Just our little good deed for you, yes?'

For a moment Fizz didn't know what to say. It sounded sort of like a good idea and it was tempting, but he knew it was wrong to lie. Even to someone who looked like Miss Toad. It didn't seem right to let these two old people tell lies for him either, even if it would get him a library card.

'I don't mean to be rude,' he said, suddenly coming up with a good excuse, 'but I think you look . . . um, well, too old to be my parents.'

'Oh!' the old lady said, as if she were surprised. She thought for a moment. 'Well,' she went on, 'we could say we're your *grandparents*. Yes, I think that when it comes to filling in forms the one is just as good as the other.'

'Are you sure?'

'Yes, absolutely,' she said. 'There'll be no trouble there.'

Thoughts of all the books in the library, all the exciting adventures that would become available for him to read, flooded through Fizz's head and washed all his worries about lying clean out. Wow! This was too good to be true. He could get his library card and his mum and dad would never need to know that he'd wandered off. Brilliant.

'Oh, thanks, that's really kind of you,' he said to the old couple. He was aware, of course, that time was drawing on and the longer he stayed away from the circus, the more likely it would be that someone would notice he was missing. 'Can we do it now? Please? I'm in a bit of a hurry.'

'Yes!' shouted the old man. His head was still cocked to one side and his eyes were shut but a big grin had sprung out from underneath his moustache. He was rubbing his hands together.

'Yes, of course we can,' the old lady added. 'By the way, before we go in, what's your name, little boy?'

'My name?'

'Yes. We'll need to know your name to fill in the forms, won't we? Must get our stories straight before we go in.'

Fizz mumbled his name so hurriedly and so quietly that it sounded a bit like, 'Fll-ll-ll Lump.'

'Pardon?' the old lady said.

She'd got a notepad and a pencil out of her handbag and was waiting to make a note.

This was where it had all gone wrong before, Fizzlebert thought. Up until he told those kids his name they'd been all friendly and kind, but the moment he'd said it out loud they'd all laughed and ran off. They'd thought it was stupid.

He didn't want the same thing to happen again. It was one thing to be laughed at by kids your own age, but to be laughed at by a pair of OAPs would take the biscuit. (Interesting phrase that: 'takes the biscuit'. I'm not sure what sort of biscuit it is that's being taken, but I'm in favour of biscuits generally and to have them taken away is never a good thing. (Unless, of course, you've eaten a whole packet already, in which case it's probably in your own best interests that they be removed.))

Suddenly a thought came into Fizz's brain, like the ping of a microwave oven saying 'this idea is now ready'.

'My name,' he said, 'is Smith. John Smith.'

(There was a rigger at the circus called John Smith and Fizz had heard him moaning about having such an ordinary name, which was probably why it had come to him at just that moment, when he needed a normal name to use.)

The old lady wrote it down on her pad and said, 'Okay. You call us "grandma" and "grandpa" and let us do the talking. You'll be a fully signed up member of the library in no time at all.'

Now, while they're going into the library and signing Fizzlebert up, I'd best have a few words with you readers. (After all, filling in forms isn't the most interesting bit of the story and I'm sure they can get on with it perfectly well without my having to describe every move.)

Fizzlebert had grown up, you must remember, surrounded by grownups. There weren't any other kids in the circus (although some of the clowns acted like kids with their makeup on). In some ways this meant he was more sensible than a lot of boys his age. He could talk to adults as if they were normal human beings and didn't feel he had to simplify things or talk slowly so they would understand. He wasn't shy. He could play several sorts of poker, lasso a runaway horse, and wasn't afraid to put his head in a lion's mouth.

However, growing up in such surroundings also meant he'd never learnt that, as a general rule, it's not a good idea to talk to strangers in the street.

Think of it this way. Every lion Fizz had ever met had been sweet and friendly and liked being scratched behind the ears. But if Fizz were to meet a lion out on the plains of Africa one day, that is to say in the wild, then he would be silly to assume that the lion would behave like the lion he had grown up with. Does that make sense?

Just because all the people he knew were adults who were also good people, it doesn't mean that all adults elsewhere are going to be so friendly and kind. (Some of them will be, but some of them won't. Some people are just mean.) And it's for this reason that you should be careful about talking to strangers, especially if you've wandered away from the circus and no one knows where you are.

While I was saying all that, Miss Toad filled in the forms and Fizz was now the owner of a brand new library card.

'You've got one book here already, Mr Smith,' Miss Toad rumbled, pointing to *The Great Zargo of Ixl-Bolth and the Flying Death Robots of Mars* which was still on her desk. 'Do you want to go choose some more before we check them out?'

'Go on little Johnnie,' said his 'grandma', 'you get yourself a couple more. What fun, eh?'

Fizz walked very quickly round to the children's section. (He did that sort of walk where really you're running, but you want everyone else to think that you're just strolling, not in any hurry, you know, all casual like, but which actually ends up looking nothing at all like walking *or* running, just a sort of rapid upright stiff-backed silliness.) He quickly picked out three other books and brought them back to the desk.

Miss Toad scanned his card and then scanned each book and stamped the due date in the front.

'There you go,' she belched, and pushed them over the counter towards him.

'Thanks,' he said, excitedly.

Tucking the books under his arm he headed for the library door, followed by his pretend grandparents. They all waved goodbye to Miss Toad who pushed her glasses back to the top of her head, popped the blue biro back in her mouth and slumped happily back down into her chair.

Once the door had trundled open and shut again and all three stood on the pavement outside Fizz said, 'Goodbye then. Thanks very much for your help, you were really kind. Thanks again.' (Like I've said before, he was a polite boy.)

The old lady leaned towards him, peering down her nose at him.

'What do you mean, "goodbye"?' she said. 'Oh dear. You can't leave us just like that, little Johnnie. You're going to have to walk us home.'

'Walk you home?'

'Yes, that's right. That's what grandsons do for their grannies, isn't it?'

'But I'm not your — '

'Oh yes you are,' she said sharply before he could finish his sentence. 'You are my grandson *now*, darling little Johnnie, and you'd better start behaving properly. I don't believe we brought you up to have manners like this.'

Fizz was confused. Was she playing a game? Was she being silly? Was she, perhaps, mad? He hadn't been worried before, but now he began to find doubts crawling around inside his head, their little spidery legs tickling his brain.

'I'm sorry,' he said, sounding braver and more confident than he felt. 'I've really got to go now. You've been really kind and I don't mean to be rude, but . . .'

'Little boy,' she hissed, leaning in so close that he could smell her pepperminty breath, 'you are coming home with us, and you are coming now.'

(There are only two reasons people eat mints: either they have something to hide; or they like mints.)

'Oh yes!' shouted the old man, punching the air. He had his eyes shut and looked as if he was listening to something no one else could hear.

'You don't know much about libraries do you?' she asked. 'Do you know what happens if you don't take a library book back on time? Do you?'

'No,' Fizz said, quietly.

'It's the cane, my boy,' she said. 'It's one smack on the palm of your hand for every hour the book is late. And you've taken four books out.'

'But . . .but,' he stuttered, 'they're not late back . . .'

'Ah, but the library is ever such a strict place. They punish you for all sorts of things. You were lucky you didn't run, weren't you? You could've been kept behind, could've been in big trouble. You're lucky you didn't make a loud noise either. You didn't know it's against the rules to chew gum or to whistle or to dance, did you? You didn't break any of those rules, because you were *lucky*. But if you had . . . oh, then you would have been in big trouble.'

'But I didn't — '

'No, you didn't. I know. But now you know what the library is really like, the sort of strictnesses they impose. So, what sort of punishment do you think they'd have if they found someone *stealing* their books? What sort, eh?'

She prodded him with a bony finger.

'Um,' he gabbled, 'a bad one?'

'Oh, yes. And look at you, my little thief. Four *stolen* books under your arm, bright as day and bold as brass. For four books they'd probably lock you up downstairs. Throw away the key. No one likes a rotten thief, do they?'

'But, I've *not* stolen – '

'Well, that depends on how you look at it,' she said, slowly running her dry wrinkled finger down the side of his face. 'Our *grandson* hasn't stolen any books, no. *He's* borrowed some books. And our *grandson* is coming home with us. If, on the other hand, you tell *anyone* that you're not our *grandson*, then your library card is *invalid*, because the forms weren't filled in correctly . . . because you *lied* to the authorities . . . and those books under your arm have *not* been borrowed. They have been *stolen* . . . and you're in big trouble indeed.' She hissed these last words right into his face. He could feel the mist of her minty spit moistening his eyeballs.

'So, what is it, John?' she said. 'Does our grandson want to come home with his poor old grandma and grandpa? Or do we have to tell Miss Toad that you are a little liar and leave you to her and her dungeon?'

Fizzlebert felt his mouth fall open and his hair go limp as he looked from this menacing old lady, to her smiling husband, to the big sign that said 'Library' (which now looked more scary than it had seemed two minutes before) and tried to work out what he could or should do now.

And I'm afraid we're going to leave poor Fizzlebert in this unpleasantly tight corner at

the end of the chapter. I have to admit, if I say so myself, it's a bit of a tense one. Crikey.

But first, I should mention (though I'm sure it goes without saying) that that old lady is telling huge lies about libraries. They're nice places, full of books and CDs and the like, and full of nice, friendly, quiet people, and the only punishment for an overdue book is a small cash fine. Even making a loud noise now and then will only get you a gentle, 'Shush please,' from the librarians.

But, as you know and I know, Fizz doesn't know any of that. He's only just found out what a library is, he's not to know they aren't as strict as this strange old lady is saying.

Oh, another thing I ought to mention now. You might be wondering why I've not told you the old lady's name (or that of her husband).

Well there's a reason for that. Her name is Mrs Hilda Stinkthrottle (and her husband's name is more or less the same, except with a Mr Arthur at the front), and there's just something about the sound of it which isn't very nice. I didn't tell you earlier because I didn't want you to prejudge her. After all, she might've turned out to be alright. Some old people are.

So there we go, that's that done, Chapter Five is now finished, all that remains for me to say is, roll on Chapter Six.

CHAPTER SIX

in which horrible things
happen and in which a remote
control is waved in the air

Mr and Mrs Stinkthrottle walked away from the library with Fizzlebert in tow. (They weren't actually towing him, they hadn't tied a rope around his neck and led him away, but the threat she had dangled over him acted in pretty much the same way.) He was forlorn and troubled and hopeless. He didn't know what else he could do.

It's all very well you saying he should have run away, because, yes, of course he should have. They were old people and old people don't run very fast, but Mrs Stinkthrottle had shown Fizz her mobile telephone (which was in her handbag). She had the library's phone number on speed dial, she said, and if he dared to make a bolt for it, she would phone them up without hesitation and then he'd be in trouble for sure. Maybe the police would have to get involved.

Fizz didn't fancy the gruesome punishments that awaited him in the library, but he also didn't fancy the punishments that might be waiting back at the circus, if they ever found out he had got into trouble at the library. His mum and dad had taught him not to lie (well, his dad had; his mum had taught him to pour

custard down people's trousers), and they'd be hugely disappointed to find out how exactly he'd gone about joining the library.

He was so confused and worried that it didn't occur to him that they'd probably be more upset to find out he'd been kidnapped by two nasty old people and taken off to who knows where in order to do who knows what.

When they eventually got to the Stinkthrottles' house Mrs Stinkthrottle opened the front door and pushed Fizz in ahead of her.

What met his eyes was awful. (What met his nose was worse, but we'll get to that shortly.)

He'd grown up in quite a small caravan in the circus and his parents had never collected a lot of stuff. Living in a little place you had

to be extra careful about that, as it could very quickly become cluttered. All you had to do was leave a couple of plates out after dinner, put a magazine down on top of them, put a half drunk cup of tea on top of that, and the next thing you knew you couldn't get through the passage to the front door (which was usually, in a caravan, the only door) without knocking it all over.

While you probably think it's a big job tidying your room when your mum nags you, Fizz didn't have that problem. He didn't have a room of his own, just a bed that folded down in the front caravan's living room, and so everyone did their bit to keep it tidy as they went along, which meant it never got out of hand.

The Stinkthrottles, however, lived in a much bigger house and they had no such

compunction. (When I first wrote that I thought a 'compunction' was a sort of small antelope, but when I checked in the dictionary I saw that it actually means 'feelings of guilt', which, now I think about it, fits the sense of what I was saying better. I should add, though, that although their house was a mess, they didn't have any small antelopes either. So my first guess was right too. A double win for me. (The author takes a bow.) Thank you very much.)

Their house looked like the set of a disaster film, just after all the big action has happened. To call it untidy would be an understatement of monstrous proportions. In fact, to call it untidy would be a bigger lie than the fib Mrs Stinkthrottle had told Fizz about the library. If there is a word that describes quite how

much like a tip their house was I don't know it (I looked), but I imagine it would be spelt with a lot more letters than just six that make up the unsatisfactory word 'untidy'.

Fizz was stood in a hallway which seemed to be made out of piles of newspapers, not just stacked up at either side (where the walls probably were), but slumped and drifting like blown snow all across the room. There was unopened post covering the carpet and when he moved his feet it all slipped and slid about. Something crunched and squeaked underfoot but even though he looked down he couldn't see what had made the noise.

There was a dead typewriter (all its keys were bent up and out of place like the legs of a dried-up woodlouse) on what he guessed was the hall table and in it was stuffed, headfirst, a

stuffed fish. It might have been a halibut, but Fizz was no expert. (If Fish was here, he'd know, Fizz thought.)

The stairs were directly in front of him and in the dim light of the hall he could see a narrow passage heading up. The once wide stairs were crowded on both sides by stacks of books and boxes and old lamps and apple cores and teddy bears and coat-hangers and wicker donkeys and crisp packets and old tomato ketchup bottles that hadn't been washed out and were now growing blue-green moulds. It was as if these old people had just dumped all their rubbish on the stairs, instead of putting it out for the dustmen.

The old couple followed him in, crowding round him in the tiny hallway, and Fizz watched as Mrs Stinkthrottle locked the front

door (three locks with three different keys, because you never can be too careful) and put the keys back into pockets hidden in the layers underneath her coat.

'Get your stupid coat off,' she said, tugging at his old red Ringmaster's jacket. 'You'd best make yourself at home, eh?'

She practically pulled him out of it and hung it on a hook on the wall, which promptly collapsed under its weight, dumping coat, hook and a shower of plaster onto the piles of rubbish on the hall floor.

'In there,' she said, indicating a door on his right with a bony pointy finger.

Fizz turned the door handle (which was sticky to the touch) and went into what must have been the lounge.

It didn't look much like a lounge. Where

the sofa would normally be was a sofa-shaped mound of screwed-up bits of paper, scrunched-up magazines, flattened cardboard boxes (for various things, such as board games, hairdryers, Cup-a-Soups and shoe-laces), ragged shreds of carrier bags, plastic bags and paper bags. In the middle of this heap were two indentations, two dips which looked to be just the right size for a pair of old people's bottoms.

Along the back of the mound-which-was-roughly-shaped-like-a-sofa was a window box (a sort of long rectangular flowerpot) out of which stuck, not flowers as you might expect, but bits of old broken crockery (all gummed up with dried or dripping food), empty bottles, a broken guitar, the type of hat a Scotsman might wear, and plenty more bits

of newspaper: in short, all sorts of rubbish. At one end a little plastic purple flower drooped drearily over the side.

Two bent bicycle wheels leant against a wall, and on a sideboard two stuffed foxes fought with a coffee percolator, a half-empty plastic milk bottle and a set of miniature suits of armour.

The rest of the front room was much the same. Plastic bags full of unidentifiable stuff piled up in the corners and the floor squelched and crunched under his feet, hidden under layers of discarded paper and who knew what. Armchairs and a coffee table sat in the usual places, but were only recognisable by their vague outlines.

And the place smelt even worse than the inside of a lion's mouth, which Fizz had

thought was the worst smell he'd ever get to know. It was a dreadful stench.

If you want an idea of the smell of the Stinkthrottles' house, here's an easy way of experiencing it via an experiment. First, ask your parents to let you take your Sunday dinner up to your room one day and instead of eating it stick it under your bed. Then, when they ask you for the plate, tell them you'll wash it up yourself and go into the kitchen and run the taps and make washing up noises and then clatter the plates in the cupboard and tell them you've put it away. And then wait. Don't wait a week, that's not nearly long enough. Don't wait a month, that's not quite long enough either. Wait for the whole of the summer holidays and then the first few weeks of the autumn term. That should be long enough.

If after all that, you're still able to go into your bedroom without being sick, I dare you to look under the bed and see what's become of that uneaten dinner.

That's *almost* what the Stinkthrottles' house smelt like. Even though from time to time they squirted a lemon-flavoured air freshener into the air, it didn't really help: the lemony freshness simply wove itself into the sickly sweet smell of rotting food and growing mould and ended up smelling slightly fishy and entirely horrible.

Fizz felt sick, and he was also scared, which made him feel even worse.

Mr Stinkthrottle took his hat and coat off and hung them up on a pile of rubbish by the door (they immediately slumped onto the floor, causing a small avalanche of rubbish to

fall down with them) and then he sat down in one of the old-person-shaped holes on the sofa.

He let out a big sigh (I won't write it out, you can probably do your own sound effects by now) and began rummaging around, as if he was looking for something.

'Go on,' Mrs Stinkthrottle said, prodding Fizz in the side with her finger, 'help him find it.'

'Find what?' Fizz asked.

'Find the remote control, for the telly,' she said, pushing him towards the sofa. 'He's only gone and lost it again, the stupid old man.'

Normally if you wanted to find a remote control you would just reach down in between the cushions of the sofa, because that's where it's usually fallen, but Fizz couldn't see any cushions, just lots of gaps in between lots of rubbish. He'd have to reach in there and he didn't like the thought of what he might find.

He pushed his hand, as carefully as he could, into a crack in the sofa-shaped pile and felt around. There was something damp down there. It was a bit like squeezing a warm sponge, only it felt lumpy as well. (Fizz remembered his mum's custard. She'd almost been kicked out of clown college

when she was younger for her lumpy custard, but her other skills (falling over without hurting herself, taking a pie in the face without flinching, walking in ridiculous shoes and so on) had been superb so she'd completed the course with pretty good grades by the end, but her custard consistency remained inconsistent. (The flavour, on the other hand, was what her Desserts Professor described as 'spot on'. (Fizz missed it awfully.)))

He pulled his hand out empty and, without looking at it, plunged it into the sofa in another spot.

This time it seemed to be a dry crevice, full of fluff and crumbs. Since his hand was sticky and wet from whatever it was he'd found on his first search, all this stuff stuck to his fingers and when he pulled them out

it looked as if he had grown fur. Colourful, crumby, crumbly fur, but fur all the same.

'Hurry up,' Mrs Stinkthrottle said, 'reach deeper. Stick your arm all the way in, go on, up to your shoulder. Have a proper rummage, sometimes it gets right to the back.'

Fizzlebert did as he was told and, with his eyes shut and his arm stretched out as far as it could go, his fingers closed around something hard and rectangular. He could feel a set of buttons on the top. This must be the remote control, he thought, and he pulled it out.

'Here it is,' he said, holding his prize aloft. (I already said in Chapter Two what 'aloft' meant, but we were in a tent at the time. This time Fizz was in a house that actually did have a loft (although, unknown to him, the Stinkthrottles always called it an attic), and this time his hand,

clutching the remote control, actually pointed towards it, so well done Fizz.)

'How dare you lie to me, your own grandmother!' Mrs Stinkthrottle snapped, snatching the object from Fizz's hand and looking at it.

When he looked round, he saw that it wasn't the remote control after all, just a mouldy chocolate bar. The squares on the top were what had felt like buttons, but now Fizz could see it, it was obvious he'd made a mistake. It was also obvious that the bar of chocolate was probably older than he was.

'I'm sorry,' he said.

'Trying to make a fool of your grandma,' the old woman said, almost talking to herself. 'What a rotten child it is.'

She looked at the chocolate bar (which was covered by a layer of lightly swaying

greenish-pink furry mould), picked a piece of feathery fluff off one end, and took a big bite.

At that moment the room filled with noise and Fizz jumped with fright. It took him a moment to realise it was just the television turning on.

Mr Stinkthrottle sat on the sofa with a big grin on his face and the remote control in his hand. He'd obviously found it down the other side of the sofa, where Fizz hadn't been looking. Because of his poor hearing the volume on the telly was up to maximum.

'Come on,' Mrs Stinkthrottle said when she'd finished the chocolate bar, 'it's time for lunch. Let's get you in the kitchen and show you what's what. What can you cook, little boy?'

Fizz couldn't cook anything, but he kept quiet and just did as he was told.

He followed the filthy Mrs Stinkthrottle's pointing finger to another door which led to the kitchen. After having seen the front room and the hall, he absolutely dreaded what the kitchen would be like.

And that's where we'll leave him for the moment. Let's have a little pause to think about what's happened. Go refresh your glass, have a sandwich or something. And then, whenever you're ready (that's the beauty of a book, it will wait for you for as long as you like), come back for Chapter Seven, which begins just over the page.

CHAPTER SEVEN

in which another boy is met and in which baked beans are cooked

When Fizz opened the kitchen door, the sight that bumped its way into his eyeballs was pretty much what he expected. The place was a mess and it smelt, though perhaps not quite as badly as the front room had, because one of the plates of glass on the back door was broken (a small square one, high up) and a tiny bit of fresh air made its way in (before promptly turning round again and going out when it met the much tougher, bullying, hard-to-get-on-with air inside).

Old Mrs Stinkthrottle gave him a sharp nasty shove from behind and he tumbled forward, landing face first on the linoleum. (Well, Fizz assumed there was lino there somewhere, underneath the food cartons, eggshells, chip grease, crushed crisps, fluff and dust, even though he couldn't see it.)

'Make us some lunch you two, we're hungry,' she snapped.

Then she shut the door leaving Fizz on his own.

Well, not quite on his own. As anyone who is paying attention to the details will have noticed, Mrs Stinkthrottle's not-so-polite request for lunch had been addressed to two

people, but Fizz wasn't paying as much attention as you and me.

Once Fizz had picked himself up off the floor (wiping dried bits of vegetable and gravy and cat food, biscuit wrappers, egg and a mysterious sweet-smelling purple slime off of himself as best as he could) he tried the back door, but it was locked. It was only after he did this that he noticed another boy in the room. He was stood next to the sink.

This boy, who was about his own age, was looking at Fizz with big round eyes from underneath a slab of blond hair. He was dressed in a grubby school uniform and held a washing up brush in one hand and a clean plate in the other.

'I was just doing the washing up,' he said in a tiny voice.

'Who are you?' Fizz asked, in a matching whisper.

'I'm Kevin,' Kevin said.

'I'm Fizz,' said Fizz, holding his hand out. (He was too distracted right then to remember to be worried about telling this boy his real name.)

'That's cool,' said Kevin taking Fizz's

hand and shaking it nervously. 'I've never met anyone called Fizz before.'

'Well,' said Fizz, 'I've never met anyone called Kevin.'

'Really?'

'Yeah. You're my first ever Kevin. I like it. It sounds exotic.'

'Really?'

'Yes, I think so.'

'Wow. At school I get picked on for being called Kevin. The other kids say it's a rubbish name.'

'Yeah, well, I like it,' Fizz said, and went on, 'But what are you doing here? How long have you been here? What happened? What are they going to do to us?'

Kevin explained that he'd been in the supermarket the day before, after school (he

went past it on his way home and his mum had asked him to pick up some milk). Mrs Stinkthrottle had spotted him and asked him for help carrying her bags. He didn't know she'd want them carried all the way home, or that she'd then ask him to take them into the kitchen and unpack them.

When he'd got there she'd locked the doors and told him to start cleaning the place.

'Why did she do that?' Fizz asked.

There was a banging from the next room and the roaring sound of the television dipped down for a second as Mrs Stinkthrottle shouted, 'Are you two cooking? Get on with it! We're hungry!' Then the telly got loud again and Kevin began to tell Fizz what he'd found out.

'Well, last night, after I'd made them

beans on toast, because that's all I can make . . . Well, they went up to bed after locking all the doors and windows. She told me to keep on cleaning. Look, I've done this whole corner over here.' (He was right, there was one corner marginally cleaner and tidier than the rest, but only marginally.) 'Well, I had a snoop around. I couldn't escape and I couldn't sleep. I was too scared, yeah?'

Fizz nodded. He didn't imagine he'd be able to sleep either, but he was impressed that Kevin had had the guts to snoop around with the Stinkthrottles asleep just upstairs. He didn't know if he would have done that.

'Well, I found this letter in the old woman's coat pocket. She left it lying on the sofa. I was looking for the keys, but she must've

taken them to bed with her. But I found this. Look . . . I reckon it must have something to do with it.'

Kevin handed him a scrunched up bit of paper that he pulled from his pocket.

'You read that while I heat up some beans. We'd best do as she says. I'm a runaway now, and you know what happens to runaways?'

Fizz shrugged and shook his head, as if to say 'No'.

'Well, the police, they lock you away. Running away from your mum and dad, even if you didn't mean to, well, that's against the law and you'll be put in prison. And I don't want to go to prison. I don't want to. She said my mum'll hate me for running off. She said Mum wouldn't even want to visit . . . wouldn't come to visit me in prison. Oh . . .

If we don't do what she says, she'll phone the police and they'll come and take me away . . .'

Kevin looked as if he were about to cry, but Fizz put his arm round his shoulder and tried to cheer him up.

'Look, it's going to be alright,' he said, not knowing if that was true or not. 'We'll escape somehow.'

'But I'll go to prison,' Kevin sniffed, still not quite crying.

'I don't know,' Fizz said by way of an answer. 'I don't know. That can't be true, can it? If we could just find your mum and dad, maybe . . .'

'But *she* said . . .'

'I know, but . . .' Fizz didn't know what to say. The thought crossed his mind that he'd run away from the circus, from *his* mum and

dad too. If what Mrs Stinkthrottle had said to Kevin *was* true, then it would apply to him too. He just didn't know.

(Of course, the whole thing about runaways being sent to prison was just another of Mrs Stinkthrottle's wicked lies, like the ones she'd told Fizz about the library. And besides, even if it was true, little Kevin hadn't *run away*, he'd been *kidnapped* by the old lady, and there's a big difference. Right now, somewhere out there, in actual fact, his mum and dad would be very worried, they'd be looking for him high and low. They might even have gone to the police, not to have him punished, but to get help in the search.)

'Do *your* mum and dad know where you are?' Kevin asked, between sniffs.

'No. They're still at the circus,' Fizz said. 'They probably don't even know I've gone.'

'At the circus? What are they doing at the circus?'

'Well, they live there, don't they?'

'At the circus?'

'Yeah, my mum's a clown.'

'A clown?' Kevin looked disbelieving. 'With the face and everything?'

'Yeah.'

'You're joking?'

'No, I'm not. That's *her* job.'

'Wow. That's brilliant. Are you a clown too?'

'No, I'm just a boy,' Fizz said.

The look on Kevin's face had changed. He no longer looked quite so scared. Now that he was distracted by thinking about Fizz's strange life, he was actually smiling.

'Does she ever let you join in?' he asked. 'I once had a clown for my birthday, but he wasn't a real clown, he was just a friend of my dad's who dressed up and did some tricks. He tried making animals out of those long balloons.'

'Oh, my mum can do that too, except she's not very good and they all come out looking like snakes.'

Kevin laughed. 'Well, this clown could only make balloon worms. He wasn't any good either.'

Fizz laughed too.

'She doesn't let me join in with the clowns very often, but last night I did the lion act with Captain Fox-Dingle.'

'Lion act?'

'Yeah, I had to put my head in Charles's mouth. Charles is Captain Fox-Dingle's lion.'

'You never!'

Kevin stared wide-eyed at him.

'I did. And I've done it before,' Fizz said proudly.

'That's amazing. Really? You stuck your head in? Weren't you scared?'

'No, not really. Charles is an old softie really. He has rubber teeth. But even if he didn't, I wouldn't worry, he'd never bite me.'

Kevin just shook his head, stunned by his new friend.

'But I'll tell you what,' Fizz added, 'his breath doesn't half stink!'

Right then there was another loud banging on the wall and Mrs Stinkthrottle shouted, 'You boys! Less chatter, more dinner! Come on, come on!'

Kevin suddenly looked serious again. The

laughter had stopped and they both remembered where they were. How they were all alone, locked in this strange house with these horrible old people.

Kevin sniffed again but quickly pulled himself together, wiped his nose on the silvery part of his school jumper's sleeve and emptied a can of baked beans into a saucepan. He popped a couple of slices of stiff stale bread in the toaster and switched it on.

Fizz looked at the letter Kevin had found in the night.

It was from the local council and, as far as Fizz could understand (a lot of it was written in long words and jargon), it said that they had received complaints from some of the Stinkthrottles' neighbours about the horrible

smells coming from their house. An inspector had been dispatched and a report had been filed which said that if the Stinkthrottles didn't sanitise (which just means clean, but *really* thoroughly) their house, the council would have to do it for them (which sounded like a good thing until . . .) and put the two old people in an old people's home while they did so. If they could get the house cleaned up themselves then that would prove to the council that they were still quite capable, thank you very much.

But it was clear to Fizz that, instead of doing it themselves, they had begun recruiting (or kidnapping) a workforce of kids to do it for them.

As the beans cooked Fizz told Kevin what he thought was going on.

'Yeah, that's what I thought too,' Kevin agreed. 'It was me yesterday, you today and who knows how many more kids she's gonna get?'

The idea was terrifying. Fizz thought of the fairytales his dad had used to tell him (his mum, not surprisingly, preferred reading nonsense poems). Kids like Hansel and Gretel got stolen away by witches, but the kids always won in the end, didn't they? But how? Fizz couldn't remember. And what he could remember wasn't much use: if he was going to stick Mrs Stinkthrottle in her own oven, he'd have to empty out the snooker balls, telephone directory, porcelain figurines and month-old remains of a roast chicken that were currently filling it up. But he didn't want to kill her (she wasn't planning on eating

him, like a witch might do), he just wanted to escape.

An idea failed to pop up with the toast, which was soon buttered with butter from the only corner of the tub that wasn't filled with crumbs and blue things (he didn't look too closely). Kevin ladled the beans on top and opened the door so they could take lunch through to the old couple.

The Stinkthrottles were sitting side by side on the sofa, each surrounded by rubbish that loomed over them, looking as if they might be buried in a landslide (a rubbishslide?) at any moment. They had trays on their laps and knives and forks in their hands, and were clearly ready for their lunch.

'At last,' Mrs Stinkthrottle shouted over

the thundering television (it was horse
racing and the hooves were pounding the
turf, and the traditional simile for that is
'like thunder' and who am I to dodge tradi-
tion?). 'You took your time about it. Give
it here.'

She really had very poor manners. Fizz
wondered how he'd ever been taken in by her.
It was only an hour or two since they'd first

met outside the library and he was amazed at the transformation.

As soon as he and Kevin had put the plates down she started shovelling her food into her mouth. (Mr Stinkthrottle on the other hand looked surprised when, a little later, he glanced down and saw his lunch had mysteriously arrived. He spooned his beans up more carefully.) In a few minutes it was all gone and she let out a small sideways burp and didn't say 'pardon'.

'You, Kevin my little one, get back in the kitchen and get on with your cleaning.' Kevin scuttled away, looking back over his shoulder at Fizz, his brand new friend, and then looking away, as if he was afraid they wouldn't see each other again. 'And you, little Johnnie,' she said, grabbing Fizzlebert sharply by the

ear and pulling herself up from the sofa, 'I've got a special job for you.'

She pulled him across the front room back towards the hallway, where they'd first come in. (Her pointy fingers hurt where they pinched the skin, and now that he'd had a chance to get a closer look he knew there was all sort of muck underneath her nails: it wasn't just the house that was dirty.) When they got to the hall she pointed up the stairs.

'Up there,' she said, 'straight in front of you, is the bathroom. I want it clean. I want it sparkling. I want it shiny. I want the mirrors so shiny I can see my face in them. Get up there. Go on. Go, go, go!'

She pushed him and he moved. He climbed the narrow passage up the stairs, squeezing

between teetering piles of rubbish, and finally found himself on the landing.

The bathroom door creaked open and he pulled the cord which turned on the light. Looking around it was obvious why Mrs Stinkthrottle hadn't washed recently.

The bathtub was full of things (the usual mix of assorted rubbish, mushrooms and discarded hat-stands), as was the sink. The walls glistened with wiggly silvery stripes, which Fizz had a feeling might have been snail trails. He didn't even want to think about looking in the toilet.

He wondered what he could possibly do to make the place cleaner or tidier (other than blow it up, perhaps).

'Get on with it. Don't dawdle,' the old crone's voice shouted from the bottom of the

stairs. 'I'll be up later to make sure you're doing it right.'

Then he heard the door to the front room slam shut. She'd gone back to her husband and the telly.

Fizzlebert was all alone upstairs, but he was thinking about poor Kevin down in the kitchen. Fizz knew that the Stinkthrottles would take ages getting up the stairs (they'd walked slowly enough coming home from the library), but they could go into the kitchen whenever they liked. Poor Kevin.

Fizz tried to think of some sort of plan of escape. He knew that he really had to now, because it wasn't just him in trouble, he wanted to help Kevin get out too. He'd made a friend that he wanted to keep. A friend he liked the idea of chatting with in the fresh air

and the sunshine outside. That made escape seem all the more urgent.

But while Fizz thinks about making daring escape plans, and works out how to make a start on cleaning the bathroom, I think it's best we take a quick break and let him concentrate without us peering over his shoulder all the time.

So, I'm going to have a lie down in a darkened room for half an hour, and then maybe a long hot bath, before I head on into Chapter Eight, which will be coming along next.

CHAPTER EIGHT

in which a search is organised and in
which a search runs into difficulties

While Fizz was trapped in the
Stinkthrottles' house, life was
going on just as normal back at the circus.

It wasn't until his mum and dad stopped for
their afternoon tea-break that they first realised they hadn't seen him around for a while.
(They'd skipped lunch, both being so engrossed
with various bits of circus business: rehearsing

their routines, obviously, but other important stuff too. His dad, for example, had his moustache trimmed by the circus barber-cum-sword swallower, and his mother did an interview for the local newspaper which ended abruptly when the reporter's notebook got eaten by Fish, the sea lion.)

At first they didn't worry too much, assuming Fizz was just in someone's caravan, but once his dad had looked all over and had come up with nothing, they began to take it more seriously. At that point his mother went straight to her caravan (only tripping over her clown shoes once and impulsively squirting the Ringmaster in the face with water when he came over to say, 'Isn't it beautiful weather today, Gloria?'). Once there she got a sponge and wiped her clown face right off.

'Okay,' she said. 'Let's go about this logically. We need to find out who last saw Fizz.'

(With her pink human face showing she was organised and sensible and anyone who saw her in action wouldn't realise how worried she was feeling. (They wouldn't have realised she was worried about Fizz if she had still been wearing her clown face either, not because she hid her worry so well, but because she looked like a clown.))

'When did you last see him?' she asked her husband.

'Well, I saw him . . .' he said, pausing to think back through his day. 'Um . . . at breakfast.'

'After that?'

'Well, he went off for his classes, didn't he?'

'Of course! Where's his timetable?'

Fizz's timetable, which listed who he saw on what day, was stuck to the little fridge door with a magnet. A quick glance at that showed that his first class had been with Dr Surprise, from ten to eleven. At 11.30 he saw Mr Bleaney, the circus's sawdust wrangler (in the circus sawdust wrangling was a very important job; outside a circus, not generally so important). After lunch he was due to visit Madame Plume de Matant, but his dad had bumped into her while he'd been looking and she'd told him Fizz hadn't turned up (which had, secretly, been a relief to her, since she *still* couldn't speak French).

'Fine, let's go see Dr Surprise first and then old Bleaney,' said his mum (who I shall call Mrs Stump, because it doesn't seem right to keep saying 'Fizz's mum' or to call

her Gloria, which was her real name, or Gloriosus, which was her clown name ('The Fumbling Gloriosus' in full)).

When Mr and Mrs Stump reached Dr Surprise's caravan, they knocked on the door.

'Hang on a moment,' a voice warbled from within. 'I'm just getting out of bed. I wasn't expecting anyone.'

'We just wanted to ask you a question,' Mr Stump said. 'Did you see Fizz this morning? Did he come for his lesson?'

'Fizz?' called the Doctor. 'Fizz?'

He sounded like he was trying to remember something, as if the name sounded somewhat familiar, but it seemed that whatever bells it was ringing were in a church tower several miles away over rolling countryside

and only the faintest of tinkles were rolling into his ears.

'Fizzlebert,' Mrs Stump called up to the window through which the conversation was taking place. 'Our son. You know him.'

Dr Surprise opened the door. He was pulling his braces up over his shirt and he had pink creases all over one side of his face, as if he'd been sleeping on something wrinkly.

'Fizzlebert?' he said. 'Describe him to me.'

'He's our boy, Dr Surprise. Don't be daft. You know him. You've known him for years. You were the doctor who delivered him.'

(Amazingly, Dr Surprise had once been a medical doctor, but that, as are so many things, is a different story entirely.)

'Ah. Now, *that* sounds familiar,' he said.

He paused and looked at Mrs Stump, as if trying to place her face. Then his own face suddenly lit up.

'Short chap?'

'Well, yes. He's a boy.'

'Your son?'

'Yes.'

'Called Fizzlebert Stump?'

'Yes.'

'That's a coincidence.'

'What?'

'I know some Stumps. They live round here somewhere.'

'Dr Surprise, that's us,' Mr Stump said impatiently. He flexed his biceps and tattoos danced across his arms.

'Oh yes, I see, of course you are. Well, I saw him just this morning, your boy.

Little Fizzlebert Stump. It all comes flood-
ing back. I remember it as if it were only
yesterday.'

'It was this morning, Doctor.'

'He came here, the small gentleman, and
we studied the great battles of history, and
then he . . .'

Dr Surprise's face stopped.

He never moved his head much, far too
professional to be animated, but up to now
he had been smiling and rolling his eyes as
if playing a game. The long loop of thin hair
that coiled round his head had been flapping
in the late afternoon breeze, and his monocle
had glinted in the sunshine. But now suddenly
that all stopped.

His hair settled.

He looked serious.

'We had our lesson,' he said, 'and then he went to the library. Are you saying that he hasn't come back yet?'

'The library? What library?' asked Mrs Stump.

'The town library.' Dr Surprise pointed in the building's direction, even though half the circus, a park, a duck pond and a row of trees lay in between. 'Didn't he tell you?'

Mr and Mrs Stump looked at each other.

'He didn't tell me,' she said. 'Did he tell you?'

'No,' he answered. 'He didn't come and find me. I was only over there, lifting a horse in the air.'

'He was returning a book. I — '

'What book?' Mrs Stump interrupted.

'It was a library book,' Dr Surprise continued. He was worried now. 'I . . . I said he should ask you. You know I would tell him that, don't you?'

'Where would Fizz get a library book?'

'He said a friend had given it to him. Something like that. Let me try to remember.'

He banged the side of his head as if it might knock loose the memory, but other than freeing some sparks which flew out of the opposite ear, it had no effect.

'A friend?' asked Mr Stump, sounding a little surprised.

'Ooh!' said Mrs Stump. 'Last night, after the show, he was talking to some local kids. They were having a laugh together. It must've belonged to one of them. They must've lent it to him.'

'It was due back tomorrow,' Dr Surprise added. 'He was going to do a good deed.'

'But he's not come back,' Mr Stump said,

looking Dr Surprise in the eyes with a look that might have been angry if it wasn't so worried.

'It's only five minutes away,' the Doctor said quietly.

In less than five minutes an expedition was

organised. Mr and Mrs Stump, along with a couple of riggers who volunteered, Dr Surprise and Captain Fox-Dingle, who needed to take Charles, the lion, for a walk anyway, started out across the park to visit the library.

Fish, the sea lion, followed along, keeping out of Charles's way, but looking hopeful.

If so many people were going in one direction, then that might be a place with fish, he thought.

Captain Fox-Dingle had Charles on a lead and he was more obedient than a dog (he was old, lazy and tired), but he did attract some strange stares from people out jogging. And he wasn't the only one. Although Mrs Stump had washed off her makeup, she (in a break with all the rules of clownery) was otherwise still in costume: a bright pink and yellow bulbous silk shape walking across the park. People stared at her too. And at Mr Stump in his strongman's leopard skin, with his little neatly oiled moustache. And at Fish, who still had his spangly silver-sequined waistcoat on. (He'd left his top hat behind.)

'It's just over here, through the trees,' Dr Surprise said, pointing the way. 'I'm a member myself.'

He got his wallet out as they walked, to show the Stumps his collection of library cards. The wallet was the sort that has little compartments for cards that fold up like a concertina and as he held it up they fluttered down to dangle in a leather strip four feet long.

'Forty-seven different library cards,' he said, proudly. 'I join up everywhere we stop. I like to read, you see.'

Mr and Mrs Stump weren't really paying very much attention to the Doctor's conversation. They were busy looking around, seeing if they could spot Fizz somewhere. There were families out enjoying late afternoon after-school picnics in the park. Every

time a boy ran by Mrs Stump's heart jumped in her chest like a giddy frog, but, of course, none of them were Fizzlebert.

After a couple of minutes they reached the library. It really wasn't very far away at all.

But it was closed.

The circus group read the times on the poster in the window. It had only been shut for ten minutes.

'What do we do now?' one of the riggers asked. 'You sure this is where he came?'

'At eleven o'clock this morning,' Mrs Stump said, dejectedly.

She didn't know what to do, what her next move should be.

She could send all her friends off in different directions, wandering the streets looking for Fizz, but would that help? Why would Fizz be on the streets? If he'd wanted to go into the town he would have asked someone to go with him. He wasn't a stupid boy. She'd brought him up properly, hadn't she? He knew not to wander off alone. But then . . .

Just as she was thinking these thoughts, trying to puzzle out an idea, Fish made a loud sea lion noise (which sounded a bit like a cross between a dog's bark and goose's honk, but smelled more of pilchard) and banged the ground with his flippers. He was pointing towards the library doors with his nose.

'Look,' Mr Stump said, 'there's someone coming.'

Mrs Stump looked through the door (the one that had opened automatically for Fizz that morning, but which hadn't opened for

his mum or dad or their friends) and she could see a figure, approaching them through the gloom of the darkened library.

It was large and it waddled. And very slowly it came closer. It was Miss Toad. She had turned all the lights off and was about to go home. She opened the door, came through, and locked it up behind her. She seemed surprisingly unsurprised to find a bunch of circus folk on her doorstep.

'Good afternoon,' she said in her voice like a burp, as she started to walk past them.

'Excuse me,' Mr Stump said, putting his enormous arm out to block her path, 'do you work here?' His arm was like the branch of a tree and she ducked to go under it. Being so short, ducking was very easy for her.

Mr Stump said, 'Excuse me,' again, and when she ignored him and walked by, he grabbed her (gently) by the collar and lifted her up. Her fat ankles paddled the air, as if they were still walking. He lifted her higher, with one arm, which was a remarkable feat since she was not the slimmest or slightest of creatures, and turned her so they faced each other.

She was, as you can imagine, a little startled by this, but as a trained librarian she did not let it show. All sorts come into libraries, especially in the winter when it's snowing outside and the library is the only free and warm building nearby. A woman like Miss Toad has to be able to deal with them, and to kick them all out at closing time. She was unflappable.

But she did stop waggling her feet.

'Excuse me,' Mr Stump said again, as politely as he could, given that he was lifting the woman in the air by the scruff of her neck. 'I just wondered if you, by any chance, work here?'

Miss Toad looked up at him through her thick glasses. Her cheeks puffed out as she chewed what was either a wad of chewing gum or the remains of her last biro.

'Yes,' she rumbled. 'Why do you want to know?'

'Our son. We're looking for him.'

'We think he came here this morning,' Mrs Stump added. 'Before lunch.'

Miss Toad thought about it for a moment and while she thought she continued chewing. Her fat round face bulged and moved as she did so and the blue ink marks round her mouth wiggled around like very weird cartoons on an even weirder television made out of skin. She blinked from behind the jam-jar-thick glasses.

'A boy?' she said eventually.

'Yes, his name is Fizzlebert. He's almost nine. He doesn't wear glasses.'

'No,' she burped. 'Not seen a boy called Filbert. Sorry.'

'Fizzlebert,' corrected Mrs Stump from behind her husband.

'Only one boy in this morning. Before lunch.'

'Well, that must have been him. Did you see where he went? Did he say anything?'

Miss Toad waited for Mr Stump to stop talking. She was still dangling at the end of his arm, but the collar of her coat had begun to stretch and her feet were almost touching the pavement.

'But,' she grumbled, 'his name wasn't Fizzlewart. It was Smith. Just plain John Smith. He told me himself, when he signed up for his library card.'

'That's a coincidence,' one of the riggers chipped in.

Mr Stump looked at him.

'Well, John,' he said, 'I don't mean to be rude, but your name's hardly unusual, is it?'

'That's why,' Mrs Stump added, 'we called Fizzlebert Fizzlebert.'

'Fizzlebert?' said Miss Toad, finally pronouncing it right.

'I mean, because it's not the same as everyone else. We wanted him to be his own person. To be unique. But now he's missing. Oh, I hope he's alright.'

She began to cry big quiet tears.

Dr Surprise produced a handkerchief from his top pocket. And another one. And another one. After a minute he had produced a string of twenty-four hankies, all different colours, and he handed her the one on the end to wipe her eyes with.

'I'm sure he'll be fine,' her husband said. 'We'll just have to keep looking.'

He put Miss Toad down (and apologised

for having picked her up) and let go of her coat. Like her namesake (that is to say, a real toad let go by a boy who'd been holding it in his hand) she just waddled by, carrying on her way as if nothing had happened, off home to have her tea and watch telly.

'Sorry about your boy, your Fizzlebert,' she belched over her shoulder as she left them. 'I hope you find him soon.'

The crowd of circus folk stood at a loose end outside the now totally shut library.

'What do we do next?' someone asked.

'Just what I said,' Mr Stump said, 'we keep on looking.'

'It's curtain up in two hours,' Dr Surprise commented.

'The show can go on without a strongman tonight. I'll keep looking until I find my boy.'

'Me too,' his wife added. 'As long as it takes.'

No one had noticed that Captain Fox-Dingle and Charles had nipped off while they were talking to Miss Toad, but just after she'd left they came back from out of the trees.

'Sorry,' the Captain said in his brisk military tone (he'd never actually been in the army, but he'd learnt a brisk officer's tone from watching war films). 'Miss anything? Charles in bushes. Bit of . . . ahem . . . call of nature. Back now. Fizz not returned? Search goes on? Yes?'

Charles roared quietly and tossed his mane about, as if agreeing.

'Yes,' the weary parents said, 'we're going to keep looking.'

'Jolly good,' the Captain said. 'Count us in. Charles likes Fizz. Head perfect size. Good show. Very good. Let's go.'

Fish eyed the lion warily and, sniffing the air, honked once as if he had an idea, but no one paid him any attention. They were too busy trying to work out a plan for the search. Who should go where? Where to look first? Should they get the police involved?

If only Fish could speak English he could have told them what it was his nose had picked up. But he couldn't speak English and no one noticed his twitching whiskers.

And so the adults began their search, and Chapter Eight comes to a close. Chapter Nine will be a good one, because we'll be back with Fizz, and I for one am quite eager to find out what's been going on in the Stinkthrottles' house.

See you there.

CHAPTER NINE

in which a bathroom is described and
in which an escape plan is formulated

You'll remember when we last saw Fizz he had just been told by Mrs Stinkthrottle to clean her bathroom, and it was a bathroom that needed cleaning.

For five minutes he just stood and looked around and wondered where to begin. He thought that he ought to make a start while he tried to come up with a plan of escape, but it wasn't until he'd emptied the sink that he thought of even the beginning of one. This (I mean emptying the sink, not the beginning of the plan) involved removing the gramophone horn (you'll have seen these, big curling cones on really old record players), the three socks (none matching), the peacock feathers, the empty mouse nest, some coal and the hairy soap.

The only way Fizz could empty the sink was to dump the stuff he took out of it into the bathtub, which was already full of all sorts of other rubbish (some of the key ingredients were mentioned at the end of Chapter Seven and I won't repeat them here). Once he had moved the junk he could see the white enamel of the sink. Well, it had once been white. Now it was stained with brown

water streaks (one of the taps dripped) and had multicoloured patches of caked-on tooth-paste and toadstools.

If Mrs Stinkthrottle really wanted him to clean the place you'd think she would have given him some cloths and some detergent, but all he had was a crumbly old bath sponge that he found in the medicine cabinet and a kitchen spatula that had been stuck to the windowsill.

He spent more than an hour emptying the sink and chipping away at the gunk and muck, before he had his idea.

It wasn't much of an idea, but it was a moment of courage. The thoughts had slowly bubbled up to the surface of his mind that he had been left alone for a whole hour, that he was alone upstairs and that the bathroom

wasn't the only room. He could, if he was really careful, sneak around a bit. Have a snoop. Have a nose about to see what he could find. It wasn't a plan of escape, but it meant he was doing something and not just giving in to the mad old woman downstairs.

At home, in the caravan, when they all went to bed his dad would lock the door. It was better safe than burgled, he used to say. He kept the key in his strongman's suit's pocket, but in case there was a fire or other emergency in the night, Fizz knew there was a spare key tucked in a sock at the back of the sock drawer.

Fizz didn't expect that the Stinkthrottles would keep a spare key in their sock drawer, he was sure that different people kept their spare keys in different places, but maybe he'd find *something*. Whatever happened, it was definitely

much better to be doing something for himself than just scrubbing a sink for her. He felt good about it, and being active even took his mind off poor Kevin stuck in the kitchen.

He pushed all thoughts of Kevin, and of his mum and dad, who he really missed, to the back of his mind. It was like having your head in the lion's mouth: you took a deep breath and tried not to think about what you were doing. Sometimes bravery is just getting on with things.

He crept across the landing on tiptoe and pushed open the first door he came to.

The room was really dark. He assumed the curtains were drawn. Either that or the rubbish was piled up so high that it had blocked the windows up. Or he'd been here much longer than he'd thought.

He ran his hand along the wall by his head until he found the light switch and flicked it.

Light filled the room, which, at a very quick glance, looked to be full of furniture, suitcases and accordions.

There was a burst of flustered flapping feathers and a loud squawking and a great clatter as two startled parrots banged their wings against their cages' walls.

Fizz's heart almost leapt out of his chest. (Which would've been a horrible sight if it wasn't just a metaphor.) He quickly switched the light off and the room was plunged back into darkness. Slowly the birds subsided. Just before he pulled the door to, one of them called him a name. The sort of name I can't repeat in a book like this (I'm far too polite, even if parrots aren't). He was glad his mother hadn't heard.

Fizz stood leant in the doorway, clutching his booming chest and listening really hard. He was afraid they'd heard the parrots' noise downstairs. But the noise of the television was still rumbling up through the floorboards and the door to the hallway hadn't opened. It seemed he'd got away with it, for now.

He decided to leave the parrots' room to the parrots, and tiptoed along the landing to the next door.

This was obviously the Stinkthrottles' bedroom. There was a thread of light from between the curtains which lit enough of the room for him to be pretty sure there wasn't any wildlife lying in wait for him.

He switched on the light.

This room, he had to admit, wasn't quite as bad as the rest of the house. It still smelt. (Of course.)

It still looked worse than even *your* bedroom looks. (Naturally.) But compared to everything else he had seen recently, it was almost tidy.

Stepping into the room he knocked against a pile of plates, and for a terrible moment he thought they were going to crash to the floor. (The bedroom was directly above the front room, where the Stinkthrottles were watching telly. They were bound to hear a bang on the ceiling.) But instead of falling they just wobbled. The plate on top was glued to the one underneath with leftover supper, and that one was stuck to the one under it, and so on down, so instead of a pile of plates, it was a column, a tower of them, and it just tilted, rocked and settled back down where it was.

The bed was unmade, and the sheets looked grey and greasy and gritty and crumby.

The pillows had indentations where the heads would lie, and one of them was stained the same blue as Mrs Stinkthrottle's hair. (She slept on the right-hand side, nearest the window, in case you wanted to know.)

Fizz left the bed well alone.

There was a dressing table, with a mirror, on one side and he had a look at what was lying about on top. There was jewellery and bottles of perfume, all of them empty. There were pots of makeup and lotions, powder-puffs and tubes of ointment. Some pepper-mints and humbugs. A book called *Forty Beauty Secrets For The Busy Woman*. (Mrs Stinkthrottle had clearly been too busy to read it.) There was nothing here that would help him and he wasn't learning anything new.

In frustration he began pulling out drawers

and rummaging. They certainly wouldn't notice any extra mess he made, so he didn't have to worry (he hoped) about putting everything back the way he'd found it. That made searching easier.

The first drawer he opened was filled with old paperback books, furry boiled sweets and a stuffed eel. The next few were mainly filled with clothes that were more made of hole than cloth. All the usual rubbish, but nothing that added up to an escape plan. And then he made an amazing discovery.

The bottom drawer was full of money.

Pardon?

The whole drawer was stuffed full of bank notes.

There was no way in the world that Fizz could count it all. It was certainly more money than he'd ever seen. It looked like it

had just been stuck in the drawer and forgotten about, except that on the top was a neat little book. When Fizz opened it he saw it was full of columns of numbers. At the bottom of each page was a figure, which he guessed was all the other numbers added up. As he flicked towards the back of the book the numbers at the bottom got bigger and bigger.

He realised that this must be the Stinkthrottles' savings. They didn't use a bank, but a bottom drawer instead.

Fizz knew about this, it was an old circus trick (and one of the reasons his dad kept the caravan locked). Because a circus is always on the move, it's hard for performers to open bank accounts, so lots of them use their bottom drawers. Fizz knew that his mum and dad's bottom drawer was nothing like the Stinkthrottles'. In

fact, his mum and dad's bottom drawer was so empty most of the time you could hear an echo when you dropped a 50p in.

Fizz stood and looked at the money (thousands and thousands of pounds, if the notebook was right) and wondered what to do. He could take it, or take some of it. If he filled his pockets up they'd never notice what was missing, would they? But what good would that do? And if Mrs Stinkthrottle looked in his pockets, or saw a five pound note sticking out, then she'd know and then he'd be in . . . well, not big trouble, he was in that already, but in *bigger* trouble, if such a thing were possible.

He put thoughts of the money out of his mind and got on with rummaging through the last few drawers, desperately looking for *anything* that might help him find a way out.

Suddenly he froze in the middle of searching. He thought he'd heard something.

Was that the downstairs door?

And then . . .

Was that the creak of the first step of the stairs?

It was. Wasn't it?

There was another creak and suddenly Fizz was sure.

Someone was coming up the stairs.

He had to run for it.

His hand was still in what was quite clearly Mr Stinkthrottle's underpants drawer. The idea of it turned Fizz's stomach, but he'd had to look everywhere. Just as he decided to run, his hand brushed against something cold and hard, something metallic. On a reflex he grabbed it and stuffed it

in his pocket, then he dashed back to the bathroom.

From the landing he could see it was Mrs Stinkthrottle returning up the stairs, but fortunately she was so bent (with her back like an upside down L, you'll remember) that she couldn't see up them very far at all. She didn't seem to notice him dart back into the bathroom.

'Johnnie? Little Johnnie,' she croaked up the stairs. 'Is it clean yet? Have you done a good job?'

'I'm getting there,' he called back, trying hard to not sound out of breath or scared. (He was both.)

'Well, you can get out now,' she snapped. 'Come out of there. Just for a moment.' (She was almost at the top of the stairs.) 'I have to use the toilet. Go on, get out.'

Fizz stood on the landing, next to the bathroom door as the top of her blue-haired head came into view. She looked pained, impatient, urgent, angry. Her face was scrunched up as if she had waited too long before deciding to get up off the sofa. She was, in short, desperate. She peered at him through the tiny glasses at the tip of her nose and her eyes were so small and pointy and mad that he had to look away and when he did he saw . . .

He saw that he'd left the bedroom light on.

If she turned around now she'd see where he'd been. He'd be for it. In big trouble.

'I've cleaned the sink, see?' he said, hoping to distract her, but he need not have worried because she just pushed past him into the bathroom and locked herself in.

'Stay there,' she shouted through the door. 'Don't move an inch. I'll be out in a minute. Oh yes, look. You're a good boy, little Johnnie, you've made that sink gleam.'

Fizz breathed a sigh of relief and put his hands in his pockets.

There was something metal in there. What was that?

He pulled out the thing he'd snatched from Mr Stinkthrottle's underpants drawer and saw it was an old pocket-watch on a long silver chain. (In the old days men would wear their watches in their waistcoat pocket, instead of on their wrists, and the chain would dangle from the pocket to a button hole where it would fasten, meaning they couldn't drop their watch and no pickpocket could steal it.) On the back there was an engraving that said,

in small curling letters: *For A.J.S. on his 21st birthday*. It had obviously been a present for someone, a long time ago by the look of it.

A pocket-watch.

Now why did that ring a bell with Fizz?

From inside the bathroom Mrs Stinkthrottle was making weird noises. There was banging and groaning and wheezing. There was

moaning and grunting and series of sounds like balloons deflating. There was one noise like ripping Velcro. Fizz didn't want to think about what she was doing. And I don't want to think about it either, so I'm going to gloss over it, except to say it wasn't going well.

Suddenly half a plan sprung into Fizz's mind. He'd remembered what it was he'd forgotten about the pocket-watch and suddenly he had a feeling of hope. The first hopeful feeling he'd had since he'd joined the library, hours and hours ago. He had a suspicion he could get Kevin and himself out of the Stinkthrottles' grasp, if only luck was on his side.

Leaving the old woman to her trials and tribulations in the bathroom, Fizz tiptoed down the stairs. He wasn't afraid Mr Stinkthrottle would hear (the telly was still

on, and the old man was, it had to be admitted, somewhat hard of hearing), but if his wife realised Fizz had gone, she'd be in a fury. He didn't want to face her if he could help it.

At the bottom of the stairs he paused in the hallway, and practised swinging the pocketwatch slowly to and fro. The trick was not to do it too quick, otherwise it wouldn't work. (There we go, that's the plan coming into sight.)

He popped the watch back in his trouser pocket and picked up his old Ringmaster's coat from the pile of plaster dust it had been dumped in when he first arrived. He tugged it on over his t-shirt and felt much more prepared, much better dressed, much more a boy of action. Much smarter, if not actually any cleaner.

Then he opened the door carefully and tiptoed his way into the front room. Old man

Stinkthrottle didn't seem to notice him. The television was still blaring away but he was sat on the sofa with his eyes shut and his head tilted to one side as if he was deep in thought. (The telly was so loud that Fizz really didn't need to tiptoe, but he did it anyway. When attempting to escape, it never hurts to be extra careful.) He crossed the room and the old man didn't open his eyes, not even when Fizz opened the kitchen door.

He crept into the kitchen and whispered Kevin's name.

Kevin was in the same clean(ish) corner he'd been in when Fizz had first met him. But now he was kneeling on the floor scrubbing it with the edge of a small frying pan. Flakes of grime and grease were flying up into the air with each thrust of the pan.

'Fizzlebert!' Kevin said in surprise. He looked pleased to see Fizz, but then his face sank and he asked, 'Did *she* send you down here? Is it time for dinner yet? I don't know what we're going to do tonight. They're all out of tins of beans and I don't know how to cook anything else.'

'No,' said Fizz, 'she's upstairs, in the . . . um, you know . . . in the loo. I've come to get you, because I think we can escape.'

'What?'

Fizz quickly told Kevin his plan.

'Do you really think you can do that?'

(Notice that I didn't tell you Fizz's plan? That's called 'maintaining the sense of suspense'. And if anyone thinks it's because I don't know Fizz's plan, well it's not. Because I do. So there.)

The two boys hurried back into the front

room. They had to be quick, because Mrs Stinkthrottle could come back downstairs at any moment and Fizz really needed to have Mr Stinkthrottle on his own.

Kevin ran over and turned the telly off while Fizz ran up to the old man, who, as you'll remember, was sat on the sofa.

He had his eyes shut, so Fizz prodded him. He would have preferred to use a stick or something (anything so as not to have to touch the old man), but he didn't have one and so he tapped his shoulder with the very tipmost tip of his finger. Mr Stinkthrottle opened his eyes and, with a puzzled frown, immediately noticed the television wasn't on. He banged the remote control on his knee and jabbed at the buttons.

Fizz stepped in between him and the telly

and the old man finally noticed him.

Our hero dangled the pocket-watch on the end of its silver chain and started swaying it back and forth.

'Look at the watch,' he said, trying to get the right calm tone that Dr Surprise always used. 'You are getting sleepy.'

Mr Stinkthrottle certainly did the first part. His eyes focussed on the shining watch face and followed it as it swung to the left and then to the right.

'You are getting sleepy,' Fizz repeated.

'What?' Mr Stinkthrottle looked up at the boy for a moment, before looking back at the watch.

'You are getting sleepy,' Fizz said, a bit louder.

'Eh?'

The old man reached up behind each of his big ears and tapped his hearing aids. There was a squeak and a whistle and then they settled down again.

'I said, "You are getting sleepy"!' shouted Fizz.

'I'm getting *what?*'

It looked so easy when Dr Surprise did it

in the show, when he'd hypnotised people and made them do his bidding. But it didn't seem to be working now. This had been Fizz's one chance, to hypnotise the old man into opening the front door. Then Kevin and he could have just run away. They'd be free. But the old man seemed to not want to be hypnotised.

Kevin nudged Fizz in the back.

'Come on,' he whispered loudly, 'is it working or not?'

Mr Stinkthrottle reached out before Fizz could answer and grabbed the watch in midswing. He held it where it was, with Fizz still holding the chain up above, and looked at it closely.

'That's my watch,' he said loudly. 'I know that watch. That's mine. I lost it ages ago. That's my missing watch! You've found my

watch.' For a moment he looked grateful, pleased to have found this thing he clearly treasured, but then his moustache quivered as if blown by an angry breeze and he snapped at Fizz: 'You're a thief! A little thief! Give me my watch back!'

Upstairs the toilet flushed.

All round the house pipes clanked and burbled and chugged, and the whole building seemed to shake. Piles of paper shifted across the floor. A plate fell off the wall and smashed. But worst of all, it was their warning that Mrs Stinkthrottle would be coming back very soon.

As the house shook, a new plan popped up inside Fizz's head. If the old man had his heart set on this watch, maybe he could use it to make some sort of bargain.

Fizz snatched the watch away. He yanked the chain so hard it flew out of Mr Stinkthrottle's snatching hands, and caught it in his own.

'If you want this back,' he said, 'open the front door. Please.'

'What? You little robber, you! Speak up,' Mr Stinkthrottle snapped, cupping his hand behind his ear to hear better.

'Just open the door, and I'll give you your watch back.'

'That's mine that is. My pocket-watch. Give it back to me!'

'Open the door, please!'

Mr Stinkthrottle made a sudden grab for the watch, but Fizz ducked out of the way. The old man followed him, surprisingly quick on his feet. He clearly wanted his watch back.

Fizz skipped a couple of steps backwards, heading towards the kitchen. This new plan was risky, but it might work. Anything was better than staying here in this horrible house with these horrible people.

Mr Stinkthrottle followed him, grabbing for the watch but always missing.

Fizz was in the kitchen and stood by the back door. When he'd first been stuck in there, at lunchtime, he'd tried the handle and knew the door was locked. But he'd also noticed that one of the panes of glass, right up at the top of the door, was broken (you can check in Chapter Seven if you don't remember).

In one quick move Fizz threw the watch through that little hole in the glass and jumped to the side.

Mr Stinkthrottle wailed, 'My watch!' and lunged at the door.

The old man rattled at the door handle, just as Fizz had when he'd first tried it. Of course it wouldn't open, but Mr Stinkthrottle stuck his hand down into his trouser pocket and began rummaging. He pulled out a stiff green hanky, and some boiled sweets fell to the floor along with some loose change and a harmonica, but suddenly there in his hand was a key.

He was so angry about his watch, this watch he'd lost and which he'd found again (in the hands of a little thief), that the thought of losing it yet again, so soon, was making his whole body shake. It took him a few tries to get the key in the keyhole, but much to Fizz's relief he did, and he promptly turned it and opened the door.

'My watch! There you are, I see you,' Mr Stinkthrottle said as he sank to his knees in the garden. He picked it up and held it to his cheek. 'Oh!'

The two boys didn't hang around. They were out the back door like fish down a waterfall.

The first thing either of them did was breathe deep of the fresh(ish) air. (The plants nearest the back door were already beginning to droop as the rotten fish and damp mould smell slumped out of the kitchen.)

The second thing they did was look round the garden to see where they could go next.

The garden was a jungle, full of brambles and stinging nettles and unexpectedly bright wild flowers. Things scuttled away in the undergrowth, rustling and squeaking. The garden was surrounded by brick walls, blocking off views of the neighbours' gardens, and the only likely path of escape was down a passage to the side of the house, which hopefully (the boys crossed their fingers) led back out to the road. They had to crawl through a few clinging, grasping bramble branches to get there, and climb over some ancient overloaded rusty dustbins in the alley, but they were so determined to escape that a few scratches and torn clothes weren't going to hold them back.

'Stop, stop!' shouted Mrs Stinkthrottle, appearing in the kitchen doorway. 'Where are you going? What are you doing? You boys! Stop!'

She'd come downstairs and found everything changed: the telly off, her husband vanished. She shouted at the boys and shouted

at Mr Stinkthrottle in the same breath, 'You stop! Come back here. And you, get up, you're just embarrassing yourself, you silly old fool!'

When she saw the boys scrabbling into the alleyway, she went back through the house moving faster than anyone would expect, and by the time they emerged from the passage out into the street she had pulled open the front door.

'Stop! Stop!' she shouted, hobbling up the front path like a bent little old lady once again.

The boys were out on the pavement and suddenly Fizz realised he had absolutely no idea where he was.

'Do you know where we are?' he asked Kevin.

Kevin shook his head.

'Just run!' they urged each other in the same breath.

As they ran off up the road Mrs Stinkthrottle reached the pavement. She was shouting, 'Stop! Thieves! Burglars! Help! They've stolen my things! My handbag, my money, my pearls! Stop them!' (More Stinkthrottle lies. Grrr.)

That was when Fizz's luck ran out. On the other side of the road a couple of burly young men were just packing up for the day after having built a wall in a neighbour's front garden. Hearing an old lady in distress, and seeing a couple of scruffy kids running away, they dropped their tools and started chasing the boys. 'Oi, you! You'd better stop! Come back here!'

What would you have done if you'd been them? I mean, what did it look like?

Fizz glanced over his shoulder as he ran and saw the men coming after them. They were both much bigger than either Fizz or Kevin and had longer legs and they were easily catching them up. Fizz put on an extra burst of speed, but he knew the race would soon be over. They'd be caught and marched straight back to Mrs Stinkthrottle.

Fizz couldn't face the thought of going back there, but his heart was pounding, his lungs were bursting and his legs were aching. Up ahead was a corner and he told himself if he could only reach that and get round it first, then maybe he'd escape for good. Maybe there'd be somewhere to hide, to duck in and dodge the men. Maybe they'd lose them and the men would just give up and go back empty-handed.

He ran.

And the corner came and he was just about to turn it when he felt a hand grab his collar, and he closed his eyes and wished he was home with his mum and dad and the rest of the circus, wished that this day had just been a bad dream. But he felt the collar of his shirt tug at his neck as a second hand grabbed his arm and he knew that this wasn't any sort of dream, except perhaps the uncomfortable and unpleasant sort known as a nightmare. He was captured. His escape attempt had failed at the last corner.

When a story stops, just at the most exciting bit and you have to wait (for any length of time) before you find out what happens, it's called a 'cliff-hanger'. Back in the old days, not just before the internet, but before people had televisions at home even, kids used to go to the cinema on a Saturday morning and they'd watch 'serial adventures'. These would always stop at the most exciting moment, usually when the hero was dangling by his fingertips off a cliff and there was no chance of escape or rescue, and all the kids would be

sure to spend their penny (or however much the cinema cost back then) the following week, just to find out what happens. And thus was born 'the cliff-hanger'. (It was catchier than the 'tied-to-the-train-tracks-just-as-the-3.47-to-Dodge-City-is-due-to-come-round-the-corner-er' which was the other name they tried.)

Which is a long way of saying, do read Chapter Ten to find out what happens to Fizz and Kevin. I don't think you'll be disappointed.

CHAPTER TEN

in which an escape is scuppered and
in which some home truths
come to light

Even as Kevin and Fizz wriggled and argued and pleaded with their captors they found themselves being marched back to the Stinkthrottles' house. As far as Frank and Tommy (the two builders who'd caught them) were concerned, there was a poor little old lady up the way shouting that she'd been robbed, and here were two lads, with torn and grubby clothes, and muck all over their hands and faces, running away. It was pretty obvious what was going on. (I don't think you can blame the builders.)

'But we didn't do anything,' Fizz shouted, desperately trying to get free from the hand that gripped his shirt. 'She's mad! You've got to believe us! You've got to help us!'

'He's right,' Kevin added. 'She locked us up. She's bonkers! Don't take us back!'

When Mrs Stinkthrottle saw the two men coming down the street with the boys, she clapped her hands and did a wrinkled little dance in delight.

'Oh, thank you!' she said. 'Thank you, you two lovely young men.'

'That's alright, Mrs,' Frank said. 'Maybe you can tell us what's going on. What have

these lads taken? Do you know these boys? Do you want us to call the cops?'

(Frank was pulling his mobile phone out of his trouser pocket.)

'They're my grandsons!' she lied, leaning back on the gate to look through her glasses at the builder. 'My grandsons. And they're rotten and lazy, but I don't think we need involve the police, not yet.'

Kevin wriggled and shouted, 'That's not true. We don't know this old woman. She's mad.'

'Now, now,' said Tommy, who was holding him tight by the shoulder. 'That's no way to talk to your gran. There's no need to be rude. Just be quiet for a bit.'

'But she's not – !'

'They were cleaning for me,' she interrupted. 'Cleaning my house, and then they

stole . . . *things*. And then they ran away. Selfish, ungrateful boys. Just give them back to me. I can deal with them from here.'

'What did they steal?' Frank asked her, then he turned to Fizz. 'You'd better give her back whatever you took. Both of you.'

'We didn't take anything,' Fizz said. 'She's been holding us prisoner. She made us into slaves. I had to scrub her bathroom. I've never met her before today. I don't know her. You've got to believe me. You've got to let us go.'

'What an imagination it has,' Mrs Stinkthrottle said. 'Just give it back to us. Poor little Johnnie. His brain must be addled. Put it back in our house and we'll deal with it.'

By now the pungent smell that oozed out of the house had become impossible for even

the politest builder (Frank was slightly more polite than Tommy) to ignore. The front door was wide open and a fishy, mouldy stink was beginning to fill the street.

'That's a bit of a pong, isn't it?' Tommy said, holding his nose.

'A pong?' Mrs Stinkthrottle repeated.

'Yeah. Coming from your hall. Have you spilt something in there?'

'Well, that's what the boys, my grandsons, that's what they were supposed to be doing, before they went *snooping* and *meddling* and *thieving*. They were supposed to be doing a tiny spot of cleaning for their poor old granny. I can't reach the high bits anymore,' she said, acting all weak and meek.

'Well then,' said Tommy, 'you two had better get on with it.'

The boys looked at each other. They didn't know what to do. All their protests had fallen on deaf ears and now they were going to be forced back into the house. If they tried to run they'd just get caught again. And neither wanted to think what Mrs Stinkthrottle would be like when that front door closed once more. She'd be livid, angry and extremely dangerous.

Frank let go of Fizz, and handed him over to the old woman.

She clutched onto his arm with her wizened claw of a hand and hissed into his ear, just loud enough so everyone heard, 'Welcome back, my little Johnnie, my little grandson. I've missed you so.'

But just as she turned and pushed him up the path towards the house, a deep thundering roaring noise burst out of nowhere.

Well, I say it burst out of nowhere, but that's only because nobody had been looking up the street: they'd all been focussed on the foul old lady and her house. But had they looked behind them they would have noticed, running down the road, a great golden shape, something like a giant dog, with a shaggy mane of hair round its shoulders.

It was, of course, Charles the circus lion, and he bounced through the little crowd of builders and boys and leapt on the old woman, pinning her to the ground.

Frank and Tommy screamed and clutched at each other and Kevin leapt out of the lion's way, landing on the pavement with a bump.

When he got up he was horrified to see that the lion had Mrs Stinkthrottle's head in his mouth. It was biting her and chewing her and tossing her about. There were disgusting wet slurping noises from the lion's mouth and deep rumbles from inside its throat. Mrs Stinkthrottle's muffled screams could hardly be heard at all. She was scratching at the beast with her dirty fingernails and kicking around with her spindly legs, but she really *was* an old woman and quite weak and so the lion hardly noticed.

Fizz was the only one who had any common sense at all, and he walked up and started stroking the lion on his neck, behind the ear like he knew he liked, and he said, 'Charlie, you'd best put her down now. She's ever so old and you might break her.'

Charles stopped banging her on the path and looked up at Fizz with big, questioning eyes, as if to say, 'Are you sure?'

Fizz looked back at the lion with a stern expression on his face and said, 'Drop!' in a firm sudden voice, like Captain Fox-Dingle used.

Grudgingly Charles lifted his head up, shut his eyes, sucked in his cheeks and spat the old woman out onto the pavement in one mighty expectoration. (Now, that's a brilliantly big word that means 'spitting something out'. I think it's my favourite word in the whole book.) She collapsed to the ground with a wet slapping thunk, her arms still wiggling and her claw-tipped fingers twitching frantically.

She lay stunned and silent on the pavement with lion saliva dribbling off her face. Her makeup was smeared all round, making her look like a felt tip drawing that's been held under a tap so all the colours run. The

dye had been drained from her hair, so that instead of being blue it was now just a plain dull grey (and a ragged mess too). Her glasses were bent and crooked on the tip of her nose and she was muttering under her breath.

The two builders were amazed and shocked.

'What? How?' they said, watching Fizz talk to the lion. They'd expected Mrs Stinkthrottle to have been killed. (They'd never seen anyone eaten by a lion before, and thought that it should have been a more deadly experience. As indeed it usually is, when rubber teeth aren't involved.) 'She's alright? How?'

'It's only Charles,' Fizz said to them. 'He's got false teeth, but don't tell anyone. He's shy about it.'

'Charles?' said Frank, not quite under-standing what was happening.

'Hilda?' said a voice from the doorway.

Mr Stinkthrottle had wandered slowly through the house (after pocketing his prized pocket-watch in the garden) until he'd reached the open front door. He had arrived just as Charles had let go of his wife.

'Hilda? What are you doing down there?' He looked at the lion. 'Is that a cat? I didn't think you liked cats, dear?'

As this was happening (the Stinkthrottles being reunited, the builders having the lion explained to them and so on) . . . As all this went on there was a commotion from further up the road.

'It's the circus,' Kevin shouted, pointing

towards the strange crowd of strange-looking people. 'The circus is coming, the circus is coming!'

And indeed it was, the whole crowd of them: Mr and Mrs Stump, Dr Surprise, Captain Fox-Dingle and the pair of riggers. And there at the front, leading them all, was the flolloping shape of Fish, the sea lion.

When we left them outside the library, they were all trying to think of a plan. Mr Stump was all for finding the local police station to get assistance, but Mrs Stump was arguing that would take too long and that they should split up and start searching the nearby streets. Captain Fox-Dingle was explaining to Charles what was going on, hoping the lion might have an idea. But before anyone could decide who should begin looking where, Fish began sniffing

the pavement, then sniffing the air, and then he wandered off snuffling along the street.

And after he had been wandering for a minute, he began flolloping, which is to a sea lion what galloping is to a horse: that is to say, top speed.

'He's got a scent,' Mr Stump had shouted, running after him.

He meant that Fish had smelt something, and was following where it led, and Mr Stump *hoped* it was the smell of Fizzlebert.

The whole crowd, including Captain Fox-Dingle and Charles, chased along behind (top flolloping speed for a sea lion (out of water) is just about jogging pace for a human), and after only ten minutes they turned the corner into the Stinkthrottles' road.

At that point Charles had heard Fizz's

voice, had heard all the commotion going on outside the house, and had recognised his friend. He'd begun to run (and running pace for a lion is a lot faster than you or I or a sea lion could run (or flollop)) and Captain Fox-Dingle was left holding the lead that Charles had broken free of.

Charles lurched off ahead, eager to help his little friend out, and pounced on the person who looked most mean, the person who had Fizz in a tight arm grip. And that's how it was that Mrs Stinkthrottle ended up underneath a lion, having her head chewed rubberly.

By the time the rest of them caught up the struggle was all over. Fizz had got Charles to let go of the old woman and Mr Stinkthrottle was helping her to her feet.

'Fizzlebert!'

(That was his mum shouting, in case you didn't recognise her voice.)

She snatched Fizz up in her arms and hugged him so tight that the rubber horn in her pocket honked.

There was more honking as Fish, who had led them all this way by following his nose, flippered up to Mr Stinkthrottle and gave him a big wet kiss. Well, that's what it looked like, but Fish was actually slapping his black tongue over the old man's face in order to get at all the leftover bits of tuna in his moustache.

He let the old man go and waddled up to the front door, sniffing the fishy air that was wafting out. (This was the smell that Fish had followed. He'd caught the scent of it almost as soon as Mrs Stinkthrottle had opened

the front door, even from as far away as the
library.) He stuck his head inside, snuffled
around and pulled the stuffed halibut out
of the dead typewriter that was sitting on

the hall table. It wasn't edible, being full of sawdust and sand, but he was able to balance it on his nose before flipping it upside down, honking, balancing it some more and finally throwing it over his shoulder into next door's front garden when he realised no one was watching.

Frank and Tommy were so surprised by the sudden arrival of the circus that for a moment they just stood there with their mouths open.

Mr Stump looked at them suspiciously.

'What have you done to Fizz?' he said, flexing his huge muscles.

'Fizz?' they said. 'Who's Fizz?'

'He is. Our son. Fizzlebert,' he said, pointing to where the corner of Fizz poked out of his mum's huge silky clown-suit-coloured embrace.

'Him? But his name's Johnnie. His granny said so.'

'His granny? How on earth did you hear from her? She's at the seaside.'

'No she isn't. She's over there.'

Tommy pointed at Mrs Stinkthrottle who was now on her feet. Her husband was holding her hand and saying, 'Hilda? Hilda? Can you hear me?' She looked dazed, and lion dribble dripped off the end of her chin.

'Gloria,' Mr Stump said, calling his wife.

'Yes dear,' she said over the top of Fizz's head, a big smile slapped across her face.

'Is that your mother there?' he said, pointing at Mrs Stinkthrottle.

'My mother?'

'Yes, this gentleman said she's Fizz's

grandmother, and she's definitely not *my* mother, so I wondered if she's *yours*?'

Mrs Stump looked at the old woman.

'No, she doesn't *look* like my mother,' she answered. 'Mum's been dead for ten years now.'

'Mum, Mum,' Fizz shouted, eagerly. 'She's a rotten old thing . . .'

And so he and Kevin, who had been carefully stroking Charles, began to explain what had been happening to them. There were gasps and tutting and much shaking of heads as the whole dreadful story unfolded.

CHAPTER ELEVEN

in which another boy puts his
head in a lion's mouth and
in which loose ends are tied up

And so we reach the last chapter of the book (that's this chapter). This is the one where things get tied up, loose ends are brushed under the carpet and I get to tell you what happened to everyone. So . . .

Once Fizz had told everyone about what the house was like inside, and about the

letter from the council threatening the Stinkthrottles with being sent away to live in a home, Tommy and Frank spoke up.

'We help my brother-in-law sometimes,' Frank said. 'He runs a cleaning company. There's nothing he likes more than a big job.'

'This is a *really* big job,' Kevin said, pointing inside. 'Have a look.'

Tommy stuck his head in the front door (covering his nose with a hankie) and had a very quick look around.

'Wow!' he said, coming out. 'That's gonna take some cleaning. Heavy duty, industrial vacuum cleaners, disinfectants, delousing . . . the works.'

'That's not gonna be cheap,' added Frank.

'They can afford it,' Fizz said.

Mrs Stinkthrottle looked at him meanly.

'No we can't,' she hissed. 'We're poor little old people. Look at us both. We've got no money and no one loves us. Everyone picks on us. It's not our fault. We got confused.'

'They're not poor at all,' Fizz said, and he told everyone about the drawer full of money in their bedroom.

'See,' Mrs Stinkthrottle snapped, waving a gnarled finger at the boy, 'I told you he was a nosey little thief.'

Mr Stump tried his very hardest to not get angry with the old lady. Still, his muscles rippled and his moustache steamed.

'If you hadn't locked my boy in your filthy house,' he said, slowly and calmly, 'he wouldn't have *had* to snoop around at all.'

Mrs Stinkthrottle muttered something under her breath and turned away.

It was just then that the police arrived.

There had been reports of a lion loose in the area and that's just the sort of thing that attracts attention. Fortunately the Captain had put Charles's lead back on and was able to produce his lion tamer's licence. Once he showed the coppers the rubber false teeth they were quite satisfied that there was no danger.

One of the first things Fizz had nervously asked his mum, when she first swept him up in her huge clown-coloured cuddle, was whether she was going to call the police. 'Why?' she'd asked, and he'd told her what Mrs Stinkthrottle had said about runaways being sent to prison. Of course, she told him it was nonsense and Fizz told Kevin and so now, when the police had actually arrived, Kevin gathered his courage and tugged one of

the copper's sleeves and told him that he was 'a lost boy'.

The policemen had heard a report just that morning back in the police station about Kevin's disappearance. He radioed immediately to say that they had found the boy. Within minutes his mum was being whisked over to where they were in a police car, with sirens blaring and blue lights spinning.

While Kevin was talking to the policeman, Mr and Mrs Stump, the Stinkthrottles and the two builder-cum-cleaners continued their conversation.

'It seems to me, Mrs Stinkthrottle,' Fizz's dad said, 'that you've got two options. Either we tell one of those policemen over there that you've abducted my son and his friend, and then you'll spend the rest of your lives in prison. Or

you can pay Tommy and Frank here, and Frank's brother-in-law, however much they need to get your house back in order, and we'll have no more funny business.' He flexed his muscles, quietly, but noticeably. 'What's it to be?'

Mrs Stinkthrottle hissed and whistled and rattled like a kettle, before she finally said, 'That's all our savings, that's all we've got! How dare you! How dare you!'

But in the end she had no choice and so she agreed to pay, and no one mentioned what had happened to the policemen. Kevin told his mum he'd got lost on the way home from school, and she was so happy to have him back that she chose to believe him.

Captain Fox-Dingle pointed out that, with the rescue done, the old people dealt with and the

police waved goodbye to, they still had half an hour to get back to the circus before the show was due to begin. Fizz asked if Kevin and his mum could have a free pair of tickets, and, of course, his parents said yes.

So, that night Kevin had the honour of walking down into the circus ring in the dazzling bright spotlight right in the middle of the show. Then, with Fizz by his side, he put his head in the lion's mouth, which made him something of a star at school the next day.

As for Fizzlebert Stump, he went back to his old circus life. He knew, however, that he'd made a friend in Kevin and every time the circus came back to that town the two of them would meet up and they'd get

together and eat toffee apples and popcorn for lunch, drink cola and sit in the lion cage telling each other about their totally different lives and their more recent adventures. And, because of the way his adventure had begun, Fizz's parents signed Fizz up to every library in each new town the circus visited (if

only to stop him trying to do it himself again).
He and Dr Surprise would go together and
borrow books, and it wasn't long before Fizz
had almost as many library cards as the mind
reader had. It was a good end to the adventure, having the freedom to read any book
you could think of. It had turned out alright
in the end.

But Fizz always wondered about *The Great
Zargo of Ixl-Bolth and the Flying Death Robots
of Mars*. In all the fear and excitement he'd
left it in Mrs Stinkthrottle's house, and it
had probably been thrown out in the big
clean. But because he'd taken it out under
the name of 'John Smith' he never got fined
when it wasn't returned. (Though John
Smith, the rigger, did get a stern letter about
it, but one of the great things about living

in a travelling circus is that it's very easy to pretend certain items of post never made it to you.)

It took more than a month for Frank and Tommy and Frank's brother-in-law to clean the Stinkthrottles' house. Frank made trip after trip to the tip, throwing out sack after sack of rubbish and junk (you can look at the descriptions in Chapters Six, Seven and Nine to get an idea of what they had throw out).

Everything had to be destroyed, all the furniture, all the curtains, the lot: it was all too rotten to keep. (Tommy tried shampooing the curtains, for example, but they just turned to rags as he touched them: too rotten and mouldy.)

Frank's brother-in-law scrubbed the walls down with industrial bleach and Tommy

killed the fleas and bedbugs that infested the place. Fortunately he had a mate who worked in the nearby city zoo, and they kindly gave a new home (with plenty of fresh air and room to stretch the old wings) to the two mangy parrots that had been shut away in the upstairs room. After a fortnight they even stopped swearing (except when they caught a glimpse of an old lady through the zoo's crowds).

The big clean was a big job indeed, but eventually it was done and the house was spotless and smelled fresh and clean once more.

All the Stinkthrottles' money had gone on the cleaning. They couldn't afford to buy new furniture and so they spent their time sitting quietly in the middle of their empty living room, on the two wooden chairs that had survived.

While Mr Stinkthrottle leant his head on one side and closed his eyes, Mrs Stinkthrottle just sat and muttered to herself. She was never quite right after Charles had sucked her head. Something in her was scared the lion would come back if she dropped some litter, even in her front room. Her eyes bulged and she kept looking over her shoulder.

For all I know, or care, they might still be sitting there now.

And that's where this book ends. *Most* of the people are happy and *everyone* has learnt valuable lessons, as they should at the end of a book. Personally, I'm not sure what the lessons are exactly, but if you were paying attention then maybe you know.